SOLE SURVIVOR

The carnage-ravaged encampment was off the trail to the right, between the fringe of the timber and a spring that was the source of a creek which ran to the west along the valley. Edge had halted his mount on the trail where it emerged from the stand of pines and he stayed in the saddle as he surveyed the fire blackened and death littered area upon which nothing moved save the gorging flies. The glinting slits of his eyes and the compressed line of his thin lips revealed nothing of his emotional reaction to the scene of slaughter and destruction. And his tone of voice was equally as dispassionate when he drawled:

"I've got no reason to hurt you, girl. But if you hold your breath much longer you could suffocate yourself."

THE EDGE SERIES:

Best-Selling Series!

#43 The Most Violent
Westerns in Print

EDGE

ARAPAHO REVENGE

BY

George G. Gilman

PINNACLE BOOKS **NEW YORK**

EDGE #43: ARAPAHO REVENGE

Copyright©1983 by George G. Gilman

A Pinnacle Book, first published in Great Britain by New English Library Limited in 1982.

First printing, November 1983

ISBN: 0-523-42041-2

Can. ISBN: 0-523-43053-1

Cover illustration by Bruce Minney

Printed in the United States of America

PINNACLE BOOKS, INC.
1430 Broadway
New York, New York 10018

9   8   7   6   5   4   3   2   1

for
V.P.
a right minded lady.

Chapter One

THE MAN called Edge finished the cigarette he had been making with slow deliberation and angled it from a side of his mouth. Then picked up the reins from where they were draped over the horn of his saddle and brought the slow walking bay gelding to a halt. He took a match from the same shirt pocket in which he carried his tobacco poke and struck it on the butt of the Frontier Colt that jutted from the holster tied down to his right thigh. Lit the cigarette, blew out the match and dropped it to the arid ground, rasped the back of a brown skinned hand over the black mixed with grey bristles on his jaw and said to his horse:

"You figure the fire under that smoke up ahead means there's a warm welcome waiting for us?"

The gelding pricked his ears to the sound of the man's voice, listening for a familiar word of command, but when none came he abandoned

1

the alert attitude and waited again in patient silence and docile passiveness for some future word or signal he could comprehend. And went through the same ear pricking and folding actions a second time when the man astride him drawled, in the same even tone as before:

"You're right. Such a crazy idea isn't worth discussing. Let's get on, and hope things have cooled down before we reach there."

He touched his heels lightly to the flanks of the gelding and the animal responded immediately, and began to move at the same easy pace as before along the trail that curved in a south western arc across the Indian Country panhandle toward the boundary line with New Mexico Territory. While Edge ceased to direct his attention exclusively toward the distant pall of black smoke—an ugly dark stain on the otherwise unmarked blueness of the mid-morning sky—and resumed his apparently casual surveillance over the terrain on every side of him.

He was riding through the foothills of the Rockies close to the southern end of the range. There were no mountains of spectacular height in this part of the country but it was nonetheless a rugged and inhospitable land over which the trail snaked, dipped and climbed. He was taking a tortuous route to avoid the steeper grades for the sake of those users who did not travel so light as the man called Edge.

But the lone rider was in no more hurry today than at any other time during the several weeks he had taken to trek from Elgin County in Wyoming to this place in Indian Country, and so did not deviate off the relatively easy path laid out by the trail to take short cuts. Swung around rearing outcrops of rock on longer detours than were sometimes necessary, ignored possible ways through strands of timber and climbed up and over ridges by the easiest rather than the shortest way.

He rode with, at the back of his mind, a firm conviction that the pall of smoke—which was neutralized into extinction some ten minutes after he first saw it—was not erupted by a fire lit for an innocent purpose. Just why he was so sure of this was not something he elected to question. And neither did he chose to speculate beyond the point of concluding that such a large cloud of smoke was not sent skywards by a single chimney or camp fire. For sometime in the near future he would come upon the scene of the blaze because, despite the circuitous route it followed, the trail he rode led toward it.

Edge smoked his cigarette down to the smallest of butts, then made certain he had pinched out every glowing ember of tobacco before he tossed it away. For he was riding across a brush-covered hillside, the young pinyon and juniper, the mesquite and greasewood, the poison ivy and the squawbush, the tomatillo and snakeweed tinder dry in this rainless fall after a long, hot summer. And he had no wish to destroy this arid wilderness—not without good reason, anyway.

This lone rider on a parched landscape under a sky the solid blueness of which was now

marred only be the dazzlingly yellow sun did
not look the kind of man to care one way or the
other about the perservation of his environ-
ment. In fact he did not seem to be the kind of
man who cared much about anything—including himself, if outward appearance was taken
as a yardstick.

He was forty and looked every day of it, having never deliberately set out to beat the ravag-
ing effects of time. Lean in his build—he weigh-
ed in the region of two hundred pounds which
were evenly distributed about his more than
six feet two inches tall frame—he was also thin
of face to the point of almost being gaunt
featured. His facial struction and skin color-
ation were the result of the mixing of the
bloods of two races in his veins—for his father
had been a Mexican and his mother came from
northern Europe. And he was dark skinned
with eyes of the lightest blue, a hawk-like nose
and a wide mouth with thin lips above a firm
jaw. His hair was no more solidly jet black for
here and there a gray strand could be seen. He
wore it long enough to brush his shoulders and
veil the nape of his neck. The dark tone of his
complexion, determined by his paternal heri-
tage, had been shaded even more by exposure
to the elements at both extremes. The lines
which were inscribed deeply into his brow, at
the sides of his eyes and over much of the
sparsely fleshed skin stretched taut between
the high cheekbones and the jaw were cut both
by the passing of the years and the harshness

of much that had been experienced during the later of these years.

To some women his face was almost repulsively ugly while many others regarded the man called Edge as sensually attractive—their opinions dependent upon how each viewed the unmistakable stamp of latent cruelty that was seen in the hooded narrowness of the ice cold glinting eyes and the set of the long, thin lips. A look which the man did not seek to emphasize by his single affectation—the way he wore the merest suggestion of a mustache that arched down at either side of his mouth. A Mexican-style mustache which, as far as he was concerned, only accidentally emphasized the Latin side of his parentage.

His mode of attire was exclusively Western American and totally lacking in frills. A black Stetson with a low crown, plain band and wide brim, a gray shirt, blue denim pants, black riding boots without spurs and a brown leather gunbelt.

The Frontier Colt in the gunbelt's holster was a standard model revolver. And there was nothing special about the Winchester rifle that nestled in the boot hung forward and on the right side of the saddle. A Western style saddle with two canteens and two bags and, tied on behind, a bedroll with a sheepskin coat lashed to the top.

Everything—the man, his mount, his clothing and his weapons and gear—more than a little the worse for wear and stained by the

dust of the countless miles of travel, stretching
back far beyond Elgin County, Wyoming.

Thus was Edge basically but adequately
equipped for traveling long trails through
tough and sometimes dangerous country—
whether the dangers be of a natural kind or
created by his fellow man. And, if the latter
should prove to be the case, he carried a third
weapon that on occasion was more effective
than a firearm. This, a straight razor that
nestled in a concealed pouch at the nape of his
neck. Hidden by his hair and his shirt and held
in place by a leather thong, strung with discolored beads, that encircled his throat. Most
days he used the blade to clean the bristles
from his face and for no other purpose. But
there were certain times . . .

He was still sure that the smoke he had seen
earlier was a danger signal, to the extent that it
signified trouble at its source. The day, moving
toward noon now, was brightly sunlit, serenely
peaceful and within the scope of his vision,
devoid of any other living thing outside of himself and his horse. A day like almost all the
others that had slipped quietly into his past as
he rode south from the slaughter in Elgin
County. During a period when his infrequent
contacts with his fellow man had always had a
mundane reason and created no bad feeling beyond nervousness and mistrust. The settlers
on their isolated places or the townspeople in
their small communities frightened by or suspicious of the glinting-eyed stranger who spoke
so few words when purchasing fresh supplies

or merely nodded and touched the brim of his hat in passing. Seldom smiling and, if he did, never allowing the expression to inject warmth into his hooded eyes. Mostly tacitly impassive, looking to be cold as high mountain ice in midwinter and hard as the rock under the glacial ice. A drifting loner who was a misfit in civilized society—be it composed of a farmer and his wife or an entire townful of people. But come totally to terms with what he was so that he was comfortable and composed in the company of others who he knew were disconcerted by his presence among them. Like he considered himself to be the only one in step. But by no means swaggeringly proud of being this. Quietly confident, though, that he was capable of asserting his rights to such individuality if anyone should call them into question.

Nobody had provoked the half-breed called Edge into a mood of aggression since that bloody sunrise back in Wyoming. Which was close to a month ago—a long time for violence to be absent from the sphere of this man who knew better than to be tempted into believing he had found peace.

The glaring but not uncomfortable hot sun had slid beyond its midday zenith when the slightly flared nostrils of the lone rider picked up the taint of old burning in the otherwise clean smelling air. He was halfway to the crest of a long and gentle rise then, his shadow and that of the gelding falling starkly black on the gray dust of the trail that was hardly distinguishable from the eroded surface of rock and

rock-hard dirt to either side. Casting dark and
truncated shadows, too, on the barren slope,
were the tops of several ponderosa pines which
were rooted on the opposite grade beyond the
ridge. But only the shade thrown by the foliage
of the pines was dark. The greenery of the tree
tops had not been charred by flames.

The gelding whinnied softly as the acrid
smell became stronger, but then calmed—
trusting the rider to take good care of him in a
time of more trouble. This intention signaled
by the gentle stroke of a hand on the neck of
the bay. Then the ugly smell of a past fire was
gone—had been wafted by a stray air current
curving over the ridge. For, halted on the crest
of the long rise, man and mount were able only
to smell the fragrance of the growing and un-
damaged pines. Which were widely scattered
over the steeper, south facing slope. The trail
snaked again now, more than doubling the distance from the top of the foot of the tree-clad
hill on this side.

Just as he had done in similar situations,
Edge started his horse downward on the trail.
Ignored the cut offs that would have shortened
considerably the time taken to get to the bottom. In no hurry to reach the scene of the
hours-old fire that was often in sight through
the widely spaced trees and thickets of brush
as he rode the curving zig-zag down the hill.

Close to the bottom land of the east to west
valley, the bay gelding whinnied his nervousness again, and was calmed by the touch of the
rider's hand. The horse perhaps once more dis-

concerted by the smell of the old fire that was now mingling with the pine fragrance in the cooler air of the timber stand. Or maybe it was the subtler and yet uglier smell of recent death that disturbed him. Whichever, the animal remained tense but quiet for the rest of the way to the base of the hill where what had once been a quite large Indian encampment was now little more than an area of scorched meadow heaped with the blackened mounds of burned-out lodges and the inert forms of the dead. The bullet-riddled bodies ranging from the youngest of papooses through boy and girl children and women of many ages to the oldest of men. More than two dozen in all. Shot in the head, the body, the limbs. Most with many more than a single blood-encrusted and fly infested wound. Patently noticeable by their absence were all the males of an age to be warriors.

The carnage-ravaged encampment was off the trail to the right, between the fringe of the timber and a spring that was the source of a creek which ran to the west along the valley. Edge had halted his mount on the trail where it emerged from the stand of pines and he stayed in the saddle as he surveyed the fire-blackened and death-littered area upon which nothing moved save the gorging flies. The glinting slits of his eyes and the compressed line of his thin lips revealed nothing of his emotional reaction to the scene of slaughter and destruction. And his tone of voice was equally as dispassionate when he drawled:

"I've got no reason to hurt you, girl. But if

you hold your breath much longer you could suffocate yourself."

One of the most beautiful women of any race he had ever seen snapped open her big eyes and stared at Edge with an expression of hatred so powerful it seemed to have a palpable force. The sound of her pent up breath rushing out through her clenched teeth carried strongly over the forty or so feet from where she lay prone among the death and destruction to the half-breed astride his horse. Less loud was the stream of sibilant words she rasped at him, sounding like a series of obscenities in her native tongue from her tone of voice that was a match for her expression of deep seated loathing.

She was in full flood when he raised a hand in a checking gesture and it took her several moments to realize the reason he did what he did. She broke off the diatribe with abruptness, but kept her expression firmly in place.

"You want to run that by me in my language, girl?" he asked as he lowered his hand back to drape the other one on the saddlehorn.

It required several more highly charged moments to pass before she had composed herself sufficiently to reply in attractively accented English:

"I said that to die is something I would rather do than to breathe from the same air as the cowardly white eyes. And that if you have a single grain of mercy within you, you will ride away from this place. So that I may die among my own Arapaho people. In a place where the evil sight and sound and smell of a white eyes does not follow me to—"

"You're a liar, girl," the half-breed cut in on her as he heeled the gelding forward. "You called me worse than a cowardly white eyes, way it sounded."

She was first angered by the interruption, then came close to being happy that Edge seemed to be starting to do what she asked. But next the anger returned, mixed in with the hatred, when he reined the gelding to a halt where the trail passed closest to her and swung wearily down from the saddle.

"You are going to finish me off?" she asked as he unhooked a canteen from his saddle. Merely hating him again.

"No," he answered and started toward her, stepping over or around the dead but uncaring that he walked through the black ashes of two burned-out lodges and their contents.

She was suddenly afraid as he halted close by her, so that his shadow fell across her craned-around head. And she blurted: "If you attempt to have pleasure with me you will catch the disease that the white eyes before you spread among we innocent—"

"Rape isn't my way, girl," he told her as he took the stopper from the canteen and dropped to his haunches. "Drink of water?"

"I want nothing from you, white eyes pig!" she snarled, and tried to spit at him. But she did not have the strength to force the globule of saliva far enough to reach his impassive face.

Edge went on, as if there had been no interruption: "See, I like my women to be the agreeable kind."

Chapter Two

THERE WAS certainly nothing agreeable about her face while she held in place the snarling expression with which she had spit at him. But she was unable to remain at this high point of emotion for long, and as she came suddenly down from it, he thought she had fainted. Because for several seconds after her head flopped to the grass and her eyes closed, her face in profile was serene in respose and her body and limbs were limp. While the gentle sounds and slight movements of her breathing were like those of somebody alseep.

In this time, Edge raked his narrowed eyes over the ground to either side of her. Saw no blood stains on the grass and looked again at the girl. Ever since he got close enough to see that she was probably no older than seventeen or eighteen he had thought of her as a girl. But from where he squatted now he found it difficult not to consider her a fully fledged woman.

And his opinion that she was among the most beautiful women he had ever seen was not altered by being at such close proximity to her.

Her eyes which she continued to keep shut for a second or so more were large and dark and round, encircled by exceptionally long lashes. And the rest of her features were in perfect proportion with these eyes and the basic structure of her oval-shaped face. Her olive brown skin was almost flawless, a tiny livid scar on her left jawline acting to enhance the girl's attractiveness by making her beauty less than perfect and therefore not awesome. Her hair was as black as her eyes, long enough to be plaited into two braids that reached to a midway point down her back.

She was about five and a half feet tall, long limbed and with a slender frame—her torso, her arms and her legs as well proportioned as were her facial features. At least, as far as Edge was able to tell, since she was fully dressed. Wore a plain rawhide shirt and skirt that encased her from throat to moccasined feet. Also unadorned by beadwork was the headband and the ribbons that controlled her hair and the bracelets at each of her wrists. She did not wear feathers nor any touch of paint.

When she flicked open her eyes, they were momentarily filled with pain. Then, for an even shorter time, she expressed shame at being seen to indulge her suffering. And immediately she worked up a fresh anger toward the half-breed.

"I do not know very many insulting names in

your language, white eyes!" she rasped through gritted teeth that were pure white and perfectly formed. "I can call you a bastard and a son of a bitch. But if you think of the worst words that one of your kind can use against another, then that is how I feel about you. You are right. When I first spoke to you it was to call you every insulting name I was able to lay tongue to in my language. But to tell you what I said in your language would serve no purpose."

"Lose something in the translation, uh?" Edge said. And offered her the canteen again. "You certain you wouldn't like a drink? Unless you took a bullet in the belly. In that case a drink can sometimes do more harm than good."

"Where I was shot is my own affair, white eyes! And I have already told you I want nothing from you! Except for you to leave me and be on your way!"

"So you can die," he said.

"That is right."

"Except when you forget your stupid pride and grimace with what's hurting you, you seem pretty healthy to me, girl."

He put the stopper back in the neck of the canteen and left it on the ground within easy reach of her as he straightened up and looked around at the bullet-sprayed and fire-razed Arapaho encampment from within it. There was no actual stink of death yet, for the babies and the children and the women and the old men had not been dead long enough during a

relatively cool fall day for their gunshot flesh
to have decomposed to the point of becoming
malodorous. But the mere fact of such whole-
sale slaughter of defenseless people contribut-
ed a certain indefinable element to the atmosphere that was otherwise permeated only by
the strong taint of old burning.

Beyond the camp site to the west, the creek
flowed in a series of sweeping curves along the
valley bottom, fast and noisily in the surrounding silence at its spring source, then more se-
dately as it lengthened and broadened. On the
other side of the camp the valley stretching to
the east was not watered by any kind of river.
Was lush with grass and timber and brush in
the area of the camp by the spring, but soon
became ruggedly rocky and aridly sandy. The
kind of terrain he had been crossing for several
days before he came over the ridge and into the
valley. On the trail that ran arrow straight
across the mile wide valley bottom and then
curved to left and right and left again to get to
the top of the high ground to the south—the
land changing from verdant to scrub desert in
this direction, too, as it rose and the distance
from the water source lengthened.

Edge took out the makings and rolled and lit
a cigarette as he made his careful survey of his
immediate and more remote surroundings. And
as he arced the dead match to the side, heard
the stopper being drawn from the neck of the
canteen. Looked down at the girl and saw she
had difficulty in raising and tipping the canteen, one-handed, to drink from it. For she con-

tinued to be in the prone position with her head twisted to the side. Like she was paralyzed everywhere except for her neck and her left arm. But her dark eyes, quick to lose the pained expression when she saw him looking down at her, challenged him not to offer her assistance.

She got some water into her throat, gagged on it, brought the expression of challenge close to being a threat and then was able to swallow the water that she now trickled into her mouth. When she had a sufficient amount, she let go of the canteen and it fell on its side so that its contents began to spill out.

"The water from the spring is cooler and sweeter, white eyes," she said after several moments when she seemed to have been waiting for Edge to speak first. "You can refill it there before you leave."

"Had it in mind to do that. Can you roll over on your back by yourself. Or do you need me to help?"

She gasped, and fear entered her eyes and compressed her lips again. "You said you would not. . . ." Tears filled and then spilled from her eyes. And the paleness of terror was more draining than that of pain that had earlier marred her natural skin tones.

"And you said you'd give me the clap if I did, girl," he told her coldly, moving to go around her and dropping down to his haunches on her blind side. "I was telling the truth and I figure you were speaking with the Arapaho forked tongue again."

"It is the white eyes—" she started, angrily defensive. But then caught her breath as she felt his hands on her.

"You can't give what you don't have, girl. And it's my guess you ain't never given the kind of performance that could get you clapped."

After her initial shocked reaction to the touch of his hands on her left shoulder and hip, the Arapaho squaw became rigid and silent. And, but for the obvious softness of the flesh beneath the rawhide of her skirt and shirt, it might have been a time-stiffened corpse that the half-breed slowly raised on to her right side then gently lowered on to her back. He, too, could well have been among the unfeeling dead, if just his darkly-burnished and heavily-bristled face was considered. For after he had voiced the wryly spoken comment his expression became entirely devoid of emotion—the ice cold manner in which he regarded the massive blood stain on the girl's shirt front, a true image of his lack of feeling over what had happened to her.

"Going to cut your shirt now," he told her while she continued to give an appearance of being dead in all save the shallow rise and fall of her blood encrusted bodice. Remained inflexibly unmoving in every other respect, with her lips compressed and her eyes—opened to their widest extent—staring fixedly up at the blue infinity of the afternoon sky. "Just like I turned you on to your back for a reason that has nothing to do with wanting to screw you,

I'm not undressing you because I think you could have the greatest pair of—"

"There were two white eyes traders," she said suddenly and, just as she kept the movements required to breathe to the very minimum, so her lips hardly moved to rasp out the words he had not invited as Edge drew the razor from the neck pouch and reached forward to begin slitting the fabric of the shirt—which could only otherwise have been removed by pulling it over her head. "They were friendly at first and offered us good deals. We trade with them and they stay with us in our camp through the night. Share our food and sleep in one of our lodges."

She gasped again, and shot the briefest of glances at his face when the cutting open of the shirt was done and he cautiously folded it back at either side. So that she felt the coolness of the air and the warmth of the sun on the now exposed flesh of her body from waist to throat. Then she gazed at the cloudless sky once more, having seen neither lust nor horror in the lean face of the man who surveyed her nakedness. His impassive expression not altered by a single line as he looked at the firm mounds of her large nippled young breasts. The right one as smoothly unblemished as the hollows of her body above and below and to the side. But the left breast was made ugly by the entry and exit wound of a bullet that had penetrated the slope of the cleavage and blasted clear of the flesh on the outer and lower slope. A great deal of blood had seeped from both holes before the congeal-

ing process was completed. There was no sight
or smell of infection yet—the discoloration to
either side of the nipple's dark aureole caused
by bruising.

"Came along the valley from the east, looks
like," Edge said to the girl as he rose to his full
height. "Aboard a four-wheeled wagon with a
four-horse team. Headed south across the valley
on the trail after they were through here."

"You can read sign as well as a brave, white
eyes," the girl said. And when this drew no response, she looked to where he had been standing. And was surprised to realize he had moved
away. "Walk as stealthily as one, too," she
added as she resumed her unblinking study of
the featureless sky immediately above her, uncaring of where he had gone and what he was
doing because there was no point in being other
than resigned to whatever he had planned for
her.

"Yeah," he responded absently from way off
to her left, over near the spring source of the
creek.

By listening intently, she was able to visual-
ize him moving about the destroyed camp,
seemingly aimlessly. But this required considerable effort which she decided was not worth
expending. And she returned to dull-toned talk
as a means of easing her pain and assuaging
her shame as she lay half naked and helpless
within the sight of a hated white man.

"At dawn, when they thought we Arapaho
were all still asleep, they attempted to make
their escape in secret. To fill their wagon with

much more than they had bartered for and to steal away. I, Nalin, raised the alarm and for this must be blamed for the slaughter that followed. The two white eyes traders had rifles. Many more than one each. Loaded and ready to be used against the women and children and old men if just such a foolish Arapaho as Nalin did as she did."

There were tears glistening in her eyes again. But they did not spill over her brown skinned cheeks this time as she continued in the same unwavering tone as before:

"The white eyes ceased what occupied them, took up their rifles from where they were kept in readiness, and began to shoot us. Without fear and with no mercy. We wanted only to ask them to treat us fairly. To give us fair trade for what they were taking. But their only answer to our entreaties was to fire their rifles at us. And not to cease firing until they were certain all of us were dead. Be they Arapaho no more than ten moons of age or more than seventy summers. All unarmed and defenseless."

"And when it was over, the white eyes continued to do as they did before I raised the alarm. As silently as before. As though we Arapaho were all still sleeping in the lodges instead of being dead outside of them under the light of the rising sun. All except Nalin who lay as if dead, entreating the Great Spirits to speed the braves back here. So that the white eyes would be captured and punished for their crimes."

"When do you expect them back, Nalin?"

Edge asked. From the trail side of the camp now.

"Perhaps before your shadow grows a grain of sand taller, Yellow Shirt will lead his warriors over the ridge and into the valley, white eyes," Nalin warned, but in a tone that lacked the conviction to give the implied threat any weight.

"Or maybe not until tomorrow or the day after tomorrow, uh?"

She blurted out a half dozen words in her own language that sounded as if they were more expletives. And then, as she ran out of dirty words—or the energy to maintain her anger—she snapped her head to the side to look toward him. For several moments she was puzzled as she watched him. Down on his haunches again, on the trail near his horse, his hands busily engaged with some chore that was hidden to her by the intervening corpse and heaps of ashes. The hardly smoked cigarette still angled from a side of his mouth, bobbing a little when he spoke.

"Hunting trip, Nalin?" he asked as he finished what had been occupying him on the ground and straightened up—lifting the lashed-together, crossed-over-ends of the two poles of a crudely fashioned travois.

"I wish to remain here to die with my own people!" she implored.

"No you don't," he countered evenly as he hooked the tied-together poles over the horn of his saddle, so that the other ends rested on the ground some five feet in back of the patiently standing gelding.

"Who are you to tell me what I do not wish for myself, white eyes?" the Arapaho girl demanded in the snarling tone of renewed, wearying anger.

"Name's Edge, Nalin. Feller more than twice your age and a whole lot uglier. Not noted for the good deeds he's done in a lousy world."

The lower ends of the poles were already linked by a length of rope. As he spoke, the half-breed began to stretch strips of canvas between the poles. The fabric, like the poles and the ropes, either charred or sooted by burning for he had salvaged all the materials from the ruins of the encampment lodges. He had to cut holes in the canvas and thread short lengths of rope through these to knot to the poles. It was a time consuming task and when the travois was at last finished it offered nothing to the eye that was rewarding. But it was serviceable.

"You do not do everything as well as an Arapaho brave, white eyes!" Nalin announced in the tone of a taunt as Edge led the gelding with the travois behind toward her. Speaking for the first time in more than the thirty minutes it had taken the half-breed to complete his work, during which she had at first watched him and then returned to gazing up at the sky.

"I haven't claimed anything for myself," Edge answered as he halted the gelding and shifted his hand from the bridle to the saddle. To reach down a charred blanket. "It's likely to hurt some when I move you."

"I hurt not at all while I am here."

She remained angry with him for a few moments more, as he squatted down at her side and covered her with the blanket. But then, as he wrapped her in the blanket from knees to armpits, lifted her and carried her to the travois, she needed to devote her entire concentration to the single aim of not giving vocal release to her pain. And for several seconds after the half-breed had lowered her into the sagging strips of canvas, she needed still to struggle against the powerful urge to scream. And was as rigid as when he touched her, large eyes screwed tightly closed, lips pressed firmly together and nostrils flared to admit and expel air with quick, rasping sounds. Until the high point of agony was scaled and she started down from it. When her lips fell apart, her eyelids flickered, her frame assumed a posture that followed the sagging lines of the canvas strips and she whispered:

"White eyes bastard son of a bitch pig."

Her eyes came wide open and a glistening tear of pain squeezed from each of them to run down her wan cheeks. She heard his footfalls and turned her head in time to see him reach the horse and hang his canteens back on the saddle, the water containers wet from being replenished at the spring.

"I say you are a white eyes bastard son of a bitch pig!" Nalin repeated, more forcefully, as Edge wiped the moisture off his hands on his pants and struck a match on his Colt butt to relight the gone-out cigarette.

"I heard," he said as he blew out the match and flicked it away. "Recall a time when anybody called me names like that would have got something different than a helping hand from me, Nalin. Don't rile so easy these days."

He slid his left foot into the stirrup and swung smoothly up astride the gelding. Glanced back and down at her to ask:

"Ready to leave?"

"No."

He heeled the horse into slow movement.

"You tell me what I have to do to make you angry enough to leave me here, white eyes?"

Edge steered the gelding carefully among the corpse and the fire razed lodges to avoid jolting the wounded girl over much and to keep from stirring up clouds of choking ashes.

"Can't do that, Nalin," he answered and, as he rode on to the trail, glanced down over his shoulder at her again. Saw that she was in pain but was withstanding it as a matter of pride.

"You are full of shit!" she forced through her fine teeth clenched together.

"Yeah," he allowed, facing front.

A minute or so later, the girl in the travois attempted: "You are a no good skunk!"

"Plus being full of shit and a white eyes bastard sonofabitch pig," he said evenly.

"Oh, why do I not know every white eyes obscenity to speak to you? Why do I not have the means and the strength to make you do what I demand? Why was I not killed like the others? Why did this white eyes not go by thinking I was dead like the others? I wished . . . ."

After she had switched from addressing Edge to making entreaties to whichever Arapaho spirit was appropriate, the venom went out of her tone and depression became her dominant emotion as she lay in the slow moving travois. To the extent where it demanded outlet in tears of hopelessness that swamped her words.

"Some days are like that, Nalin," Edge said against the soft sounds of her sobs. "Just one lousy thing after another."

Once more he looked back and down at her pathetically frail looking, blanket-wrapped form cradled in the crudely made travois. And she was abrubtly shamed again, to be seen with tears coursing over her cheeks. Hurriedly, and not without pain that was revealed in a series of wincing grimaces, she drew both arms from within the blanket and fisted her hands to rub the salt moisture from her red-rimmed eyes and pale cheeks.

"Since I do not know the words to say to you, white eyes, I have nothing to say to you!" she told him, with a tone of disdain that entirely negated the tear ravaged look of despair on her beautiful young face.

"That's okay," Edge answered as the gelding started up the first curve of the trail out of the valley. "Won't make any odds to the horse, I guess. But if you quit with the talk, to me you won't be so much of a drag."

Chapter Three

THE GIRL spat out a stream of Arapaho obscenities as the half-breed turned to face front again. But quickly tired of drawing no response from him—or was exhausted by this new bout of ineffective rage. And fell into a silence that was as private as the one in which the man had wrapped himself.

In recent times there were just two words which would arouse a vicious anger within the man called Edge. *Mex* or *greaser*—whether they be spoken of him or anybody else with Mexican blood in their veins. And a man or woman who used either of these derogatory terms within earshot of the half-breed was certain to suffer for the sun. Just as surely as anybody who drew a gun against him twice after being warned the first time was doomed to die.

Perhaps, he was prepared to admit, he had some other idiocyncrasies. But none to which

his reactions were so consistent. It had not always been thus—the rules by which he lived his
life so clear cut. Paradoxically, when he had
been a simple farmer on the Iowa prairie, he
was a far more complex personality.

He had been Josiah C. Hedges then, working
alongside his crippled younger brother to make
of the farmstead what their parents—buried on
the property—had wanted it to be. Until the
War Between the States erupted in the east
with effects that reverberated across the entire
country. There was little soul-searching to be
done on the small Iowa farm. And there were
no recriminations between the brothers anyway—after Joe left to become a Union cavalry
officer while Jamie stayed.

Neighbors were inclined to say that the kid
had the worst of it. Having to work the place all
on his own at such a tender age and with a
game leg—shattered by a bullet fired accidentally by his elder brother several years earlier.
And, maybe if he had been pressed on the
point, Joe Hedges would have allowed those
neighbors could well be right. For there could
have been few occasions during the years of
war when Jamie enjoyed himself, toiling for
long and lonely day after day to beat nature
and his infirmity just to keep the place going
until his brother returned—or the Department
of War letter arrived to say it had all been for
nothing. While on the blood-soaked, explosion-
shattered, black powder smoke-cloaked battle-
grounds of the east, Joe came to relish evading
the death that would have caused such a letter

to be mailed to Iowa—and to revel in the countless acts of killing before he was killed.

The first half of the eighteen sixties was a
time of terror and anguish, pain and despair,
hatred and tears—for almost every man,
woman and child touched directly or at a distance by the bloody Civil War. And, in truth,
Lieutenant and later Captain Josiah C. Hedges
experienced his share of the darker human feelings at the very outset. Before the first founda-
tion stone of the man he was to become was
laid and quickly built upon.

Then the war was ended and like hundreds of
thousands of other youngsters become men in
the worst of all worlds, Joe Hedges was instructed to abandon the values he had been set
and to pick up where he left off before he
answered his country's call to arms. And, he
had always maintained, he was prepared to do
this when he turned his back on the uneasily
peaceful east and rode toward the Midwest—
where the elements and an occasional band of
renegade Indians should have been the only
enemies. But he arrived home to find Jamie
dead and the farmstead a burned-out ruin. And
vengeance had to be exacted before life without
resort to the gun could be recommenced.

And vengeance was exacted, Joe Hedges
using all his war-taught skills to achieve this.
But in killing Jamie's killers, he stepped across
a line that had not existed in time of war. And
became a wanted murderer with a price on his
head. And also, by the mispronunciation of his
name, he came to be the man named Edge.

He was no longer a wanted murderer. He was no more certain that, even had Jamie been alive and the farmstead was a halcyon haven, he could have stayed on the place and worked it. Married and raised some kids, maybe.

He did get married. And tried to revert to being Josiah C. Hedges. In the Dakotas rather than in Iowa. But on a place of similar size and potential. Had known, he could lately acknowledge, that the life he had sought to make for himself and for Beth was as doomed as that it had been in his mind to live when he rode back home from the war.

He used to blame fate for all the hardships and deprivations he was forced to endure. Then himself for creating the situations in which he grasped what he wanted only to have it snatched away from him.

Until he came to realize that if life was the total of what he wanted, he could never again be made to suffer the anguish of losing what was near and dear. Unless there was life after death, which was an area he had no wish to theorize upon.

"White eyes?" the Arapaho girl called in a weary tone when they were halfway to the top of the valley's southern slope, moving at a measured pace over the sign left by the four-wheeled rig and four-horse team.

"Yeah?"

"You do not look the kind of man who does good deeds out of the kindness of a heart he does not have."

"I told you I wasn't noted for that, Nalin."

"I think you do not do anything for nothing."

"I do what I do."

"That says nothing."

"You're the one wants to talk."

"For many hours I lay where I had fallen at our camp, white eyes. At first pretending I was dead while the murderers stole from the lodges and the bodies and then made the fires of the lodges. Hardly daring to breathe for fear they would see the movement and kill me. You know this?"

"Only way for you to survive, Nalin."

"That is why you say I lie when I claim I wish to die among my people?"

"No."

She had begun to sound confident. Now a timbre of irritation was in her tone again when she snapped:

"That you are old and ugly I will not argue, white eyes! But that does not give you right to tell me what to think."

"You're seventeen, Nalin. Or maybe eighteen?"

"In my eighteenth summer, but that does not make any difference."

"Girl of seventeen should only have to decide how to wear her hair or what color dress to put on. Worry how far to let her beau go. Stuff like that."

"White eyes girls in safe white eyes towns, perhaps!" the Arapaho squaw snarled. "But I am Indian! More foolish than any of your white eyes girls perhaps. Who by her foolishness is to be blamed for the slaughter of so many of her people!"

"Everybody's done things they wished they hadn't. But there's no way to turn back the clock. And if there were, somebody else would probably have done the same wrong thing."

"Then I would be among the dead!" she countered in a triumphant tone. "As I wish to be now."

"And maybe I'd have a quieter passenger to haul, girl. And a more grateful one."

"Grateful, you white eyes bastard son of a bitch pig?" she hurled up at his broad back. "What do you mean? I did not ask to be here! I tell you all the time I wish to be left with my people! It is for yourself that you have brought me with you! Although you say it is not! If I was dead at the encampment and an ugly old squaw or an elder of the band was alive, I do not think you would be going to this trouble!"

They had reached the southern ridge and Edge reined in the gelding on the rocky and almost barren high point. Turned from the waist to rake his narrow-eyed gaze in every direction, seeking a sign other than that of the wagon and the Arapaho encampment that there was human presence beyond himself and the girl in this piece of country. And in the clear, sunlit air of late afternoon saw nothing of the band of Arapaho braves nor the treacherous white traders who had wrought such carnage at their camp.

To the east, the unwatered stretch of valley

petered out on to a high plain of sand ridges, rock outcrops and sagebrush thickets. While the western length of valley, with the spring fed creek become a river, swung to the south and then the east in a gigantic half circle. And although it was not possible to see the glint of sun sparkling water because of the intervening country, it seemed likely that the trail and the river came close to each other again in the far distance. The nature of this country spread to the south was predominantly rocky. Not rugged, though—the rises and outcrops and small mesas smoothly surfaced, and curved rather than angled. Close to the ridge that was his vantage point, the terrain was almost totally lacking in vegetation. But gradually, as the half-breed's gaze raked closer toward the far off return curve of the river valley, he saw the land become increasingly verdant and timber clad.

"This isn't Arapaho country, Nalin," he said when he was certain they were alone for as far as any human eye could see.

She was momentarily confused by his sudden change of subject and answered without pause for thought: "Yellow Shirt and his band have been dispossessed by the white eyes and—"

"You were all just passing through," Edge put in.

"In search of a place to live in peace," she answered, on the defensive.

"You come across Calendar?"

"Calendar?"

"It's a town. The next one along this trail a
trapper told me awhile ago."

"We do not go to the white eyes towns. We
know we will not be welcome there."

"Crazy old trapper likewise. He'd just heard
of the place and couldn't say how far away it
was."

He started the gelding moving again, at the
same slow pace as before. And the girl, who had
begun to appreciate the relief of the short stopover, took perhaps a whole minute to get used
to the discomfort of being on the move again.
Before she asked dejectedly:

"Why you take me to this place, white eyes?"

"Because you're with me and I need to visit
town, Nalin. Buy some fresh supplies."

She was silent again, for less time and for a
different reason. Blurted out the accusation at
the end of pause for thought:

"To buy what you need with money from selling me? There is a house of pleasure in this
town of Calendar and you will sell me to the
people there! I will be forced to—"

"Nalin," Edge cut in evenly on the girl as her
voice began to rise in pitch and volume toward
the point of hysteria.

"—be used by white eyes men for money that
will be paid to—"

"Nalin!" the half-breed snarled, as he reined
in the gelding and swung fast in the saddle, the
sudden stop and his abrupt change in tone
startling her into frightened silence. He nodded
shortly as he fixed his gaze on that from her

much bigger and darker eyes—each seeing the other upsidedown because of their relative positions. "You're young, you're beautiful and when that gunshot wound heals you could be the best thing that ever happened in any cat house. Especially since you appear to have the kind of mind that's so concerned with screwing."

"I do not—" she started to protest.

"Just shut up for awhile and listen, uh? If you weren't hurt and I went with whores and you were up for screwing at a bordello, I'd maybe pick you. Same as if you weren't hurt and you made yourself available to me because you liked my looks, I wouldn't kick you out of my bedroll, Nalin. But none of that is here nor there. You had a bad time this morning. Saw a lot of your people slaughtered and blame yourself for what happened to them. Had to play dead for God knows how long to keep from getting finished off yourself. Then couldn't move for a whole lot longer, out of fear of pain until I—"

"Neither fear nor pain, white eyes!" she challenged. "I was ashamed ·and filled with remorse. I remained where I had fallen among my dead and rotting people, entreating the Great Spirits to end my life, too. I must be punished for what I did."

"Okay, Nalin," Edge allowed, facing front and starting the gelding forward again. "Not only are you a beautiful and screwable young lady, you're real brave and you can take pain without cracking."

"White eyes bastard son of a bitch pig," she rasped softly.

"And you have a guilty conscience," he went on, unperturbed by the latest interruption.

"You have no conscience, I think!"

"Maybe, maybe not. But I've got certain rules I live by, Nalin. Not too many, but enough so I can sleep easy when there's no other reason to stay awake. And I figure I'd wind up real weary if I sold a woman to a cat house."

She did not reply for a very long time now. Over a period during which the sun dipped low enough down the south western dome of the sky for the air to get noticeably cooler. While the only sounds were the clop of the gelding's hooves, the creak of the saddle leather and the slithering of the travois poles over the dusty ground.

Then she said, in a strangely subdued tone: "I am not new to the ways of the white eyes."

"You didn't learn to speak our language out of an old primer," Edge acknowledged as he worked his sheepskin coat free of the bedroll. "It's getting cold. You want some more blankets around you?"

"No. Thank you. I was orphaned by a sickness when I was very young. And was taken and raised by an Indian agent and his wife. Mr. Hart did not remain Indian agent. Went to Kansas City and bought dry goods store. I went to school in Kansas City and lived almost like a white eyes. Until I can no longer endure being almost like a white eyes. And run away.

Three summers ago. With sorrow for Mr. and Mrs. Hart who had helped me so much. But I think they, too, were suffering much that I was just almost like a white eyes."

Edge had on the topcoat now, the collar turned up to brush the underside of his hat brim and the buttons fastened to the waist. The sun was changing hue from yellow toward crimson and he made full use of the light as it faded to survey their distant surroundings. But the only living things to be seen were birds. None of them buzzards.

"You sure you don't need extra warmth, Nalin?"

"No. Mr. Hart, he was something like you, Mr. Edge." It was the first time she had spoken his name, but she used it without any inhibition. "And many other white eyes men, I know. He would not have allowed me to make up my own mind and do what I decided, either. Because I am young." Her voice had begun to take on an embittered tone and now she paused to compose herself, as if afraid she would lose his attention if she did not retain her self-control. "I am sorry. I was wrong to accuse that you are helping me only because I am a female who is pleasing for a man to look upon. But I do not think I was wrong to say that if it was an old squaw left alive, you would not encumber yourself with her. And delay your arrival in this town of Calendar to which you go? If she asked you to leave her there to die? An old squaw or an elder of the band? Even a young brave, perhaps?"

"Maybe, maybe not," Edge said again.

She made a sound of disgust deep in her throat, like she was gathering saliva into her mouth to spit. But she did not spit and nor did she have anything more to say as evening came with its gloom to replace the light of day in the wake of the setting sun. And just the sounds of the horse, the saddle and the travois disturbed the massive silence. A stillness, beyond the slow moving group to which the half-breed listened as intently as he had watched his surroundings before darkness dropped over them.

But he heard nothing that caused him to move a hand away from the reins toward revolver or rifle. And it was his eyes which picked up the first sign that Nalin and he were no longer alone within the confines of their horizons—limits on all sides reduced by the coming of night. And then, to the south, extended by a pinprick of light. A light that glinted, coming and going so that it resembled the effect of a star in the distant haze. But too low to be this, beneath the black on black of the uneven skyline.

The Arapaho girl sensed the sudden rise and fall of tension in Edge and asked, a little fearfully: "Something is wrong?"

"Light ahead. Long way off."

"Fire?"

"More like a lamp."

"Not moving?"

"That's right. From a window."

Nalin gasped. "Or the cover of a wagon, perhaps?"

"See how much fun staying alive can be, girl?

When you maybe have the chance to hurt who-ever hurt you?"

She gasped again, then retorted in bitter tones: "It is not for my sake I am here!"

"You asked, I told you."

"Not a wagon, you think?"

"I'd bet on a lamp in back of a window, Nalin."

She sighed. "You are a white eyes and so are they. I am Arapaho. You are a man and they are men. I am hurt and unarmed. It would not matter if those two murderers of my people were behind the light ahead."

Edge made no reply as he rode the horse trailing the travois down a sloping length of the trail that put the glimmer of light out of his angle of vision. And he was content with the silence between them, while sensing that she was sullenly resentful. Some fifteen minutes later, after the lamplit window had come and gone from sight a number of times, and the man in the saddle had rolled and lit a cigarette, the girl riding uncomfortably behind said in a melancholic tone:

"I am sorry, white eyes."

"What did you do now?"

"You are right."

"I try to be."

"Please let me finish! You are right concern-ing the eagerness I felt when I thought the murderers of my people might be close by. It is perhaps worth the humiliation of my position to know that I might have the chance to make them pay for what they did."

"No charge, Nalin."

"This I do not believe, white eyes."

"You don't?"

"It has already been said. A man like you, he does nothing for nothing."

"That's fine."

"What is?"

"That since you've gotten over being so mad at me, you figure I did you some kind of favor."

"Ah," she exclaimed, triumphant again. "And since you do nothing for nothing, you will expect to be repaid—in some way?"

"Something else has already been said. No charge."

"Not in money, of course, white eyes. And you have no use for my body. But there will be something you will need from me. And when the time comes for me to make the decision, I will not feel it necessary to explain to you why I do as I do."

Her silence was expectant now, and when he failed to fill it with the explanation she had invited, she vented a sound of exasperation and demanded: "You heard what I say, white eyes?"

"Sure."

"And have nothing to say?"

"If I had something worth saying, I guess there's nobody better suited to it, Nalin," he drawled past the cigarette bobbing at the side of his mouth.

"I do not know what you mean," she answered, intrigued.

"Getting a word in Edgewise."

Chapter Four

THE LIGHT which appeared and went from sight very many times during the next two hours was at a window in a building on the north bank of the river that had its source in the valley where the slaughter of the Arapaho had taken place.

The valley existed as no more than a broad indentation in the landscape at the point where the trail reached the half mile wide, slow rolling river—was really an expansive plain between the low and increasingly gentle area of hill country through which the half-breed and the girl had come and a range of jagged ridged mountains perhaps as much as a hundred miles to the south, the flatland not commencing until the far side of the river.

Nalin said nothing during the slow trek through the hills until Edge reined in the horse and swung down from the saddle. After which, the soft sounds made by the gently flowing river could be heard. And the girl asked, in a tense and nervous whisper:

"What is it?"

"A house. At a ferry. You want to take a look?"

"I would."

Edge moved to the rear of the gelding and looked closely at the Arapaho girl for the first time since he had loaded her on the travois. She looked sicker and weaker and in more pain— perhaps because of the bluish tinge that the moonlight gave to her skin. But after he had got her out of the travois, asking for and receiving no help from the girl, she was able to stand unaided. Gripping the blanket around her shoulders like a shawl as she peered toward the house, a hundred yards along the trail.

It was a two story, frame built house with a low pitch roof. Built directly onto the western side of the trail some twenty yards back from the river bank, where a pier as wide as the trail jutted out into the water. The ferry boat, which was nothing more than a log raft long and wide enough to accommodate a wagon and four-horse team with a rope rail at either side, was moored fore and aft alongside the pier.

"Why you people stop back there?" a man who spoke English with a stronger accent than Nalin called.

And caused both Edge and the girl to wrench their gazes from the crudely constructed ferry to the house which a long time ago had been a fine home, before the combined effects of the elements and neglect had attacked its timbers and paint and glass. So that now, from the viewpoint of Edge and Nalin, the only window that was not broken and boarded up was the one with the light in back of it. There was an unpatched hole in the roof shingles and the stoop had collapsed along almost its full length. Not a single square inch of any part of the building's fabric gleamed with recent painting. And there was a dry smell of decay emanating from the place.

"Either of the traders talk like that?" the half-breed asked of the girl as he directed his unblinking gaze at the boarded up window from which the query had been shouted—on the other side of the door to the window that continued to spill lamplight across the trail.

"No," she answered and there was still fear in her voice. But she released the grip she had fastened tightly to his arm when the man had announced his presence in the house.

"You want to get across the river, Maziol will take you! Fifty cents for each passenger! The horse is for nothing!"

He sounded foreign, elderly and eager to please—perhaps frightened and ingratiatingly anxious to perform his service and be rid of the strangers. Maybe a little drunk.

"You live alone here, feller?" Edge wanted to know.

"Yes, yes! Maziol the Frenchman has lived alone all his life in your country!"

"Can you walk?" the half-breed asked of the girl, while he continued to watch the house.

"I think so."

He went along the side of the horse on the right and took hold of the bridle with his left hand. Murmured a word of encouragement to the animal and then led him over what was left of the trail to reach the front of the house. He could hear the moccasined feet of the wounded and weakened young girl shuffling and dragging on the ground behind him. He halted immediately outside the door of the house, ten feet from it, in the wedge of light from the window. Looking and listening and ready to respond in a split second to the merest hint of the suspected threat being proved.

"Hey, why do you act like there is something to be afraid of at Maziol's place?" the man behind the boarded up window asked, sounding even more nervous now. "You are making me frightened, you know that?"

"I know that," Edge answered. "But you have nothing to worry about, feller. If you just step outside and take us over the river."

"Sure, sure. I will do that. It is why I am here."

The door and flanking windows were all in the front wall of the same room. Edge could see the light in the crack at the foot of the door— and also between two boards at the broken window after Maziol moved away. Two bolts had to be shot before the door could be dragged open on its sagging hinges and the ferryman stepped across the threshold and halted abruptly. Frowning his terror as a sound from behind him caused the tall, lean man on the trail to become visibly tense, obviously within a hairsbreadth of streaking a hand to his holstered revolver.

"Alone but for my mules, *monsieur!*" Maziol shrieked, his gaze held firmly in the trap of that from the slitted, lamplight glinting eyes of Edge.

Then the animal-like snort sounded again and the Frenchman bent slightly back from the waist, at the same angle as the half-breed leaned toward him. And Maziol uttered a choked cry of alarm as Edge sniffed—smelling the maleodorous air that was wafting out of the doorway behind the frightened man. Air strongly permeated with the stinks of animal droppings and wet.

Nalin came to a halt alongside Edge and vented a tense laugh of relieved tension. Which drew the gaze of the ferryman toward her, his fear also suddenly draining away as he eyed the Arapaho girl's beautiful young face and undisguised appreciation.

Edge growled: "Mules? In the house?"

"Some people I have known had dogs or cats or cage birds in their houses," the Frenchman answered, smiling now as he shifted his gaze up and down Nalin, apparently assessing the shape of her body beneath the shawl-like blanket.

He was about sixty, a match for the half-breed's height but much thinner in build and face. He was almost bald, with just a half circle of gray hair around the back and sides of his ridged skull. The skin hung on his face was crinkled and mottled. He had small, deep set eyes and a small mouth under a prominant nose. Bristles sprouted patchily over his lower face and throat, like some areas of the skin were dead. His hands and feet were bare and filthy. His pants and the upper portion of his longjohns were patched and darned in many places.

"And, of course," Maziol went on after he had completed his survey of the girl and vented a soft sound of approval, "the most fortunate men of all get to share their houses with a woman. Although few have the good fortune to be favored with a woman as beautiful as this. She belongs to you, *monsieur?*"

"No, feller."

The ferryman had showed little of his decayed teeth when he had first smiled. But now he displayed their discolored lengths from uneven tops to shrunken gums as he blurted excitedly:

"She is not for sale?"

"Yeah," Edge told him evenly.

And the girl vented a gasp of shock and flinched away from him as her eyes, with reproach displayed by horror, turned their stare from the Frenchman to the half-breed.

"How much you want for her?" The Frenchman's deep set dark eyes glittered almost as diamond brightly as those of Edge.

"Yeah, she ain't for sale, feller."

Nalin sighed, but continued to hate the Frenchman—and also Edge for causing her this latest experience with fear. And she murmured bitterly and hardly audibly:

"White eyes bastard son of a bitch pig."

While Maziol struggled to conceal the extent of the anger he was feeling toward the other man.

Edge said: "You want the dollar in advance, feller?"

The ferryman came close to losing the temper he was suppressing only by tensing every muscle in his body. And this showed in the robot-like stiffness of the way he swung around and was heard in the harshness of his tone when he muttered:

"You pay me when we get to the other side, *monsieur.* I will put on my boots. You will prefer to wait outside the house, I think?"

"Yeah, we prefer to wait outside," Edge answered.

The tall, thin, ugly, bad smelling ferryman re-entered his badly neglected house that gave shelter to himself and his animals. And made more noise than was necessary, to the accompaniment of a string of obscene sounding words in his native language, as soon as he was out of sight of the couple out on the trail.

"Perhaps the mess made by the mules inside does not smell so bad—" the Arapaho girl started to say as she peered across the threshold of the now empty doorway. But cut short the intended taunt against Edge when she sensed, rather than saw, that he had moved suddenly away from the side of the gelding.

She snapped her head to the side, big eyes widening to their fullest extent as she saw where he had gone and what he had in mind to do. And her mouth was suddenly also gaping

wide, to give vent to a sream of terror and
horror when a gasp from the doorway caused
her to wrench her attention back there. In time
to see the emaciated and dissipated Maziol
start out of the house in a lunging run—canted
forward from the waist and with both arms
held stiffly down so that his hands were at the
same level as his knees. Both hands clenched,
the left one fisted around the butt of a revolver
and the right to the handle of a long-bladed,
one-sided, sharply-pointed knife. While on his
slackly skinned face with its strange pattern of
bristles and areas of dead looking tissue was an
expression of lustful evil intent that lasted for
no more than a half second—the time it took for
the Frenchman to see that Edge was no longer
standing in an attitude of apparent casual indifference beside the beautiful young Arapaho
girl.

In that time, he saw not only that the half-
breed was out of sight. He saw, also, the horrified expression which abruptly became fixed to
Nalin's lovely face, and the direction in which
her gaze had gone to look at Edge. Then the
gun exploded. Perhaps with an intentional shot
or maybe because it was old and had a sensitive
action that was triggered by accident out of
fear as Maziol faced up to the unknown conse-
quences of his error of judgement. Whichever,
the elderly Navy Colt discharged a bullet that
missed the head of the suddenly screaming girl
and entered the head of the bay gelding below
and behind the animal's right eye. To kill him

in an instant before it was deformed under the top of the skull.

What had started as a gasp of alarm in the throat of the Frenchman was suddenly a shrill shriek of mortal fear. For the momentum of his lunge could not be halted and he was across the threshold, his leading foot among the weather and termite ravaged timbers of the collapsed stoop. Going through the rapid motion of thumbing back the hammer of the Colt while certain it would be to no avail. Just as he made to turn the knife and his body in the futile hope of plunging the long blade into a vulnerable area of the half-breed's belly or chest.

It was to the right side of the doorway, from the man's point of view, that Maziol turned the knife, his body and his head. And started to swing the half-cocked Colt, too. But froze in the part turn, the sound of terror dying on his lips as the Frontier Colt of Edge drew a bead on his face—the revolver in the brown skinned hand held out at arms length with the unwavering muzzle just an inch from the bridge of the petrified man's nose. The half-breed's left hand held the threat while he remained flattened to the front wall of the house beside the door, head turned so that he could sight along the rigid length of his arm and the barrel of the gun into the ugly face of Maziol.

The dead horse made no sound outside of those of his collapse to the hard packed trail as he died. And in the immediate wake of this series of thuds there was a moment of utter silence that was almost painful in its intensity. Until Edge said flatly:

"At least the horse was well shod, feller."

"Pardon?" Maziol answered, pronouncing the single word to make it from his own language. And opened both his hands, to release the knife and the gun—winced when the butt of the big Colt banged him hard on the bare left foot.

"Out here in this country, it's supposed to be better to die with your boots on, feller."

Both the Frenchman and the Arapaho girl caught their breath—he held in the frozen attitude still while she straightened up after almost hurling herself to the ground when the horse was shot.

"Monsieur, I am no longer armed!" Maziol squeezed out of his fear-constricted throat. And some saliva trickled out over his lips with the words.

"You want to answer me a question?" Edge asked as he folded away from the wall while he kept the gun firmly aimed at the pale face of the Frenchman.

And it was almost as if there was an invisible extension to the barrel of the revolver to which the man's head was skewered. For Maziol moved only his small eyes in their sockets to seek the girl and plead:

"Mademoiselle, I am an evil man! Perhaps driven mad by the loneliness of my wretched existence at this place where my skill with the ferry is called upon so seldom! I beg your for-

giveness and ask humbly that you tell the man
with you to please spare my life! You are so
beautiful and it has been so long for Maziol! I
was a fool but I do not deserve to die for this!
You will please speak to him, *mademoiselle*? I
have nothing to offer but my gratitude! But in
the hours and days and weeks and years to
come you will always think well of yourself for
saving the life of an unfortunate soul who was
so moved by your beauty that he came close to
death to—"

"Frenchman," Edge cut in, his tone of voice
and his expression still totally lacking in
emotion. And, when the small, fear-filled eyes
redirected their attention, he went on: "There
ain't no way you can give an answer unless you
listen to the question."

"You cannot kill such a pathetic old man,
Edge." Nalin said.

"You will spare me if I answer truthfully,
monsieur?" Maziol asked eagerly.

"Have you seen a bunch of Arapaho braves
around here recently, feller?" Edge countered.

The Frenchman appeared to want to shake
his head vigorously, but could not move it even
fractionally in front of the gun in the rock
steady fist. He blurted, as eagerly as he had
pleaded his case to the girl:

"*Non, monsieur!* I know of the band you
speak of, though! They are to the north of here
so you have missed them! I ferried two men
across the river this afternoon! Men who trade
with the Indians! They have on their wagon

many artifacts for which they have bartered
with Arapaho band! The *mademoiselle*, she is
lost from her people and you are seeking to
return her to them! My shame is the greater to
know that I considered adding to the suffering
of this poor lost creature! How may I—"

At his mention of the two traders who he had
taken across the river, Nalin turned to peer in
the direction they had gone—and began to
mutter a string of obvious invectives across
the night-cloaked country in their wake.

"Much obliged, feller," Edge said and although there was no change in his tone or his
expression, the Frenchman knew it was almost
over for him. Sensed the approach of death as
those who are mortally sick can sometimes feel
how close they are to the end.

"But I answered you truthfully!" the doomed man wailed, and tears spilled from his small
eyes. "You must spare me!"

He raised his hands, elbows close to his sides,
palms uppermost and fingers splayed.

"Promise you one thing, feller."

Nalin now became aware of impending death
and curtailed her cursing of the two men far
beyond the river to stare with awe at the two
just a few feet from her.

"*Monsieur?*" Maziol managed to force
through his discolored teeth as little more than
a rasping exhalation of his breath.

"Treat your mules better than you treated
my horse."

The Frenchman brought up both his hands,

fingers still splayed but curled into hooks now to fasten over the Frontier Colt and the wrist behind the hand fisted around the butt. Although his eyes continued to glisten with the tears of the doomed, his face was contorted into a gargoylish expression of depthless hatred for the man who was to kill him. So that he looked not quite human during the two seconds it took him to fasten his grip and drag down on the gun and the hand that held the gun.

Then Edge, whose total impassiveness was in its way inhuman to behold, squeezed the trigger of the revolver. And kept his arm rigidly out in front of him as the Frenchman tightened his double-handed grip—needing the support of the half-breed to remain on his feet as the strength went out of him. Draining from his muscles as fast as the blood that gushed from the exit wound at the back of his neck. And then he was dead, the shock of his nervous system of the point blank range shot—tunneling the bullet into, through and out of his flesh killing him long before he would have drowned in his own blood or been suffocated by his inability to breathe.

His hands released their grip and his arms fell to his sides. He thudded down hard onto his knees and his thighs folded toward his calves. But his head lolled to the right and this acted to alter the direction of the fall—caused him to sprawl out onto his side across the threshold of his foul smelling house.

The half-breed had lowered his left arm by

this time, and had brought across his right hand to thumb open the loading gate of the Colt so he could tilt the gun and turn the cylinder to extract the spent cartridge case. While he did this, the Arapaho girl, a look of revulsion distorting her beauty, muttered sour words in her own language. Then she recalled Edge could not understand what she was saying and translated:

"To kill him like that, you are no better than those who slaughtered my people. I know he tried to kill you. And that if he had done so, it would have been bad for me. But to shoot him down like that. . . ."

She could not think how to finish this in English. And allowed a shudder that shook her from head to toe to express her feelings. This as Edge slid a fresh shell into the chamber and returned the Colt to the holster tied down to his right thigh, then dropped to his haunches, gripped one of the Frenchman's wrists and rose. Backed away to drag the corpse out of the doorway.

"You have nothing to say, white eyes?" she demanded when he had let go of the lax wrist which thudded back to the ground.

"Not for me, not for you, girl," he answered flatly, and shifted the gaze of his hooded, glinting eyes from the shocked face of the Arapaho squaw to the dead gelding in back of her.

"Just because your horse—" she began.

And Edge drew back his thin lips to display his teeth in a vicious grin that gave him the look of an animal about to bay in triumph at the kill. Instead, he rasped softly:

"I got a frog in the throat."

Chapter Five

THERE WAS an ancient buckboard parked at the side of the house facing the river, the rig as neglected as the house and the man who had owned both of them. Its timbers were dry and warped, its metalwork was rusty, one of its wheels was buckled from having a broken spoke and its axles and springs creaked from lack of greasing. But it rolled without collapsing and the harness was good enough to take the strain of the wagon, two people and the gear of one of these. Hauled by a pair of mules who, unusual for their kind, went to work with a will. First took kindly to being led from the spartanly furnished house and hitched to the buckboard. Then moved obediently out on to the pier. Waited patiently for Edge to cast off one mooring line so that the raft-like ferry swung around on the sluggish current until it was end-on to the pier, when they moved without instruction to roll the wagon aboard, re-

sponding to familiar circumstances without
need of orders.

Perhaps there was, in their dark eyes, a look
of pointed contempt for the manner in which
the half-breed propelled and steered the raft
out into midstream, by regularly thrusting a
long pole into the riverbed and applying all his
weight to it—moving to left or right across the
stern when the ungainly craft threatened to
come about. This while Nalin sat like a carved
statue on the seat of the buckboard, gazing stoically ahead and seemingly uncaring about the
progress and direction of the ferry. But then,
when it became apparent the craft would not
dock at the pier on the south bank, she turned
to look at the stone-faced man on the stern with
the same kind of expression he was certain he
had seen in the eyes of the mules each time he
did something that Maziol had done differently.

The river flowed serenely from west to east
and the ferry went in the same direction so that
it was very soon obvious that the craft would
reach the opposite shore a considerable way
downstream of the pier. For a full minute, perhaps, while Edge moved back and forth on the
stern and raked his glinting-eyed gaze over a
long length of moonlit river bank in search of
the probable landing point, the young girl continued to peer over her blanket-draped shoulder toward him. And he tried to devote his entire
attention to his chore, pretending he was not
aware of her disdainful surveillance.

Until he felt too irritated to ignore her

further and growled, raucous against the gentle rippling of the water around the ferry: "An Indian would make a better job of it, uh?"

"No, I do not think so, white eyes," she answered, and winced as the act of turning on the seat started a worse pain in the area of her bullet wound. She had moved to look beyond the man on the stern, toward the house with the door still open and light spilling out over the abandoned corpse of Maziol. "But I think an Arapaho would have waited until the man with the skill to get the boat across the river had done so. Then would have killed him."

She shifted the direction of her gaze again, to look back at the half-breed. And both her tone and her expression brightened to reveal she felt she had scored a point against him.

"Lot of white men would have done the same thing," Edge allowed in an easy tone of voice that spread a frown across the face of Nalin. "But that ain't my way."

"The difficult way is the foolish way when there is an easy way!" she challenged, on the defensive.

"Figured it was easier to kill him for shooting my horse, Nalin," he answered, evenly. And paused to change the direction of his pacing of the stern, but added before she could voice an objection: "Than it would have been for helping me cross the river."

She seemed on the point of countering his argument, but then decided either that she had nothing valid to say or would be wasting her breath to say it. Which irritated her into turn-

ing too suddenly to face front again. And a cry
of pain burst from her lips. Or, Edge allowed, it
could have been a sound of alarm that the ferry
seemed about to hit a rocky point on the bank.
But he had spotted the danger before this, and
was prepared to avoid it—by thrusting the pole
hard into the riverbed from the side instead of
the stern of the ferry. So that the bow came
around, perhaps ten feet short of impact. At
which point the half-breed exerted his full
strength against the pole. And it ceased to be
an axis on which the raft turned and became
the means by which the ferry was propelled
into a narrow inlet with the rocky area on one
side and a stand of willows on the other. The
entrance just half as wide as the raft while the
strip of water beyond was twice as long as the
ferry, which scraped the bottom and was firmly
aground before the stern was free of the gentle
but insistent tug of the river current.

Edge abandoned the pole now and it floated
away downstream. And climbed up on the
buckboard seat, conscious that the Arapaho
girl was ready to direct taunting scorn at him
for the least mistake.

"Going to be a rough ride for awhile," he
warned as he took up the reins and kicked at
the brake lever.

Nalin took a firm grip on the handrail at the
side and on the backrest of the seat as she nodded shortly and then replied: "I have learned to
expect nothing more from you!"

She had to shout the final few words, to make
herself heard above the yelling voice of Edge

and then the din of the mules and the wagon
lunging into motion. And as she did so, she
frowned darkly at him, misinterpreting the
reason for the grin that was suddenly fixed to
his lean features. Thinking he was enjoying her
pain and fear as revenge for some barbed comment she had made and to which he had not
previously responded. Whereas he was expressing his pleasure the way in which the mules
obeyed his demands.

He had made an educated guess that they
would. After being confined within the house
on the far side of the river for so long, they had
shown themselves eager for exercise and freedom during the few minutes it had taken to
harness them to the buckboard and drive them
onto the ferry. But mules being the obstinate
natured animals they were—maybe as volatile
in temperament as women . . .

The mules started forward like two quarter-
horses trained for sprint racing. Off the bow of
the grounded raft and into the shallow water of
the inlet. To drop perhaps two feet to the surface and another foot to the muddy bed beneath. When they snorted and flailed in terror
of the unexpected—and sought to bolt clear of
the unfamiliar.

The buckboard went off the bow and the girl
screamed, as terrified as the mules, when her
handhold on the backrest was torn free at the
sudden forward tilt of the rig. And she would
have been thrown off the wagon and into the
water—perhaps to be crushed into the bed of
the inlet by a wheel—had not Edge flung out

his right arm to clasp her around the waist.

The rear wheels of the rig came clear of the
bow to crash down into the inlet amid an explosion of spray. And the backwash acted to speed
the progress of the ferry out into the river, the
raft having become free of the bottom when it
was relieved of the buckboard's weight.

While the mules, not liking the sucking softness of the mud struggled to the limit of their
strength to get clear. Urged on additionally by
the snarling voice of the half-breed who knew
that, if they stalled, the wheels of the wagon
were likely to sink deeply into the mud and
remain firmly stuck there. But this was a
potential danger for just a few stretched seconds before the animals and then the wagon
were thudding and jolting across a rock strewn
pebble shore, shedding water but fully out of it.
And, as with the ferry raft earlier, Edge
abandoned his attempts to keep the mules
moving to concentrate upon steering them.
Which was not easy, since high timber in back
of the riverside stand of willows blocked out
the moon and the panicked mules were for a
long time deaf to his voice and unresponsive to
the reins as they raced blindly over the danger-
ously darkness-clad ground. Seemingly, it was
easy to be certain of, hauling the buckboard
along a course that caused its wheels to find
every hollow, bump and loose obstacle between
the timber on the left and the bluff that had
suddenly loomed to the right.

But at least he had both hands on the reins
now, having completely encircled Nalin with

his right arm to achieve this, so that her
slender body was held tight against him. And
he could hear her venting more words in her
own language. But whether she was cursing
him—or the circumstances—or was pleading to
her God for deliverance he had neither the opportunity nor the inclination to decide. The rig
pitched and rolled, jerked and jolted and if it
did not cant too far and tip over there was a
danger of a wheel collapsing. Directly ahead
was just a dark unknown and since the bolting
mules refused to be halted by the dictates of
the man with the reins, all he could do was keep
them racing into the unknown. Which could be
no more dangerous than the trees to one side
and the rock face on the other. While he waited
for a sudden collision or for the failing strength
of the mules to slow the headlong pace and
bring it to a gentle halt.

And it was the latter alternative that ruled.
Signaled by a stumble by the animal on the
right that could well have led to a crash had the
mule not righted himself. And Edge gave the
team a free rein, but used the brake—cautiously applying and releasing the blocks against
the wheelrims to increase the burden of the
tiring animals.

The clatter and thud and creak of the high
speed run gradually became less to the accompaniment of the regular shriek of the brakes.
And then the reduction in the pace could be
seen as well as heard. The man and the girl became suddenly aware of each other again—
Nalin to pull away from Edge's embrace and he

to release her without a struggle. They felt the sodden wetness of their clothing from the spray when the wagon had hit the water. Experienced, too, the tackier moisture of sweat both beneath their clothing and on their exposed faces as it was suddenly chilled and dried. The buckboard was just seconds away from rolling to a halt behind the sweat lathered, snorthing and trembling mules. And the man and the girl were able to look about themselves. To recognize that they were in a ravine with a cliff to either side, but the bluff to the east hidden for most of its length by a band of pine. Ahead, the way was no more veiled by darkness. For the ground began to rise, the trees to the left as tall as ever but the facing cliff losing height, toward a moonlit area where the ravine ended.

The rig came to a standstill and the heavy breathing and the snorts of the exhausted mules were the only sounds to disturb the peace of the night for stretched seconds. Before Edge leaned to the side and spat. And Nalin asked tensely:

"Something in your mouth taste bad, white eyes?"

"Never known fear to taste good."

"It is a fool who is never afraid," she allowed, less strained but not ingratiating in her attitude.

"It also ain't smart to go without food and rest unless you have to."

"I do not think I can eat. But to be still on the ground and not on something that is moving—I would have no objection."

There was ample kindling and fuel for a fire in the timber and an ample supply of water for coffee and cooking at the river. But when the fire was burning steadily, emanating pleasing warmth to keep the increasing chill of the night at bay, Edge elected to use the spring water from his canteens rather than make the more than a mile round trip to the river. And within an hour of hitching the mules as the first act of making camp, he and the Arapaho girl were sharing a mug of coffee and the smell of boiling salt meat was wafting appetizingly out of the cooking pot.

There had been no talk while Nalin remained up on the seat of the buckboard, huddled in the blanket, and Edge undertook all the chores. But the silence was not a strained one although the half-breed—sound in health and as sure in the circumstances as he could be that he was in command of his own destiny—was undemonstratively more contented than the Indian girl who tried not always with success to hide her pain and weakness.

When she handed him back the mug after taking a second drink of the coffee, it was she who spoke first, to end a period in which he had always signaled a query and she had either nodded or shaken her head. She said evenly:

"Yellow Shirt and the braves came to the south, Edge. When they left the rest of us at the camp beside the spring. But they were far to the west of the trail."

"They left no word with you when they'd come back?"

"The females in our culture are not made

privy to . . . Oh, I see what you mean. Not me personally?"

"Whichever," he said as he struck a match on the Colt butt to light a fresh rolled cigarette and extended the mug of coffee toward her again.

She accepted the coffee with a nod, drank some of it and gave it back. "The elders were told and I think some of the squaws found out what was said. But I knew nothing. Although I am a full blood Arapaho who has never been guilty of breaking the laws of my nation, I am never trusted as I would be had I not been raised for so long as a white eyes by the Harts." She shrugged, her wound momentarily forgotten but then winced as it was painfully recalled.

"I don't carry medical supplies, Nalin," Edge said. "If you want me to, I'll bathe it for you. Maybe that'll ease the pain. Maybe needs to be cleaned anyway. Help to keep it from getting infected."

The girl was briefly perturbed that he had seen her react to the stab of pain. Then was intrigued and eyed him levelly as she tried to decide if she was right or wrong about this man's strangely unfamiliar demeanor. And when, as he finished talking and leaned forward to stir the contents of the cooking pot, she reached the conclusion she was correct. The attention he gave to the food was an excuse to avert his eyes, but he should have looked away from her a moment earlier. Before she saw that he was uncomfortably embarrassed. Which was a state of mind, she felt sure, he did not experience often.

"It is all right, white eyes," she said softly and smiled her understanding at him as he continued to give his attention to the good smelling contents of the cooking pot. "After so much rough riding, my wound does not pain me so badly as it might, I think. Just when I forget it and move too suddenly. So it is not poisoned, I am sure."

She released her grip on the blanket at her throat and looked down at the bullet holed breast partially revealed by the razor cut shirt. But made sure that, if Edge glanced at her, he could not see her body in the flickering light of the fire—shielded herself with the blanket.

"It looks okay, as well as feeling okay?" he asked and when she wrapped the blanket around her body again she saw that he was looking at her through the drifting smoke of his slightly moving cigarette. "Sometimes when a wound doesn't hurt it can be a bad sign."

She nodded her agreement with this and needed to make an effort to remain unsmiling at the half-breed's continued discomfiture. "Yes. But it is not so with me. I am young, and I think that young flesh is quicker to heal than old."

"Yeah," he answered. Cleared his throat and offered: "You want some more coffee?"

She nodded and felt free to smile now as he refilled the mug from the pot and handed it to her, signaling with a hand gesture that he

wanted no more before the meal. And she said:
"I think I will have some food, too. I was not
hungry at first, but the smell of what is cooking has changed that."

"That's good," he replied absently and
another vocal silence fell between them. Edge
seeming somehow relieved by it while the Arapaho girl appeared eager to end it. But came to
the point of speaking several times, only to
check the impulse—like she felt it important to
raise the right subject or could not determine
just how to broach the subject she had in mind.
Until the half-breed offered her the first serv-
ing of food on their only plate, and she waved
for him to eat it while she finished the coffee.
When, as soon as he had tossed away his cigarette and taken a first mouthful of meat, she
opened:

"I must thank you, white . . . Edge."

She had begun to peer across the top of the
steaming mug into the fire. Now shot a side-
long glance at him and saw the tacit query in
the glinting slits of his ice cold eyes as he
chewed at his food with no show of relish.

"Not just for bringing me with you," she
went on, returning her dark-eyed gaze to the
fire. "But for taking such good care of me as
well. And for not taking . . . for not using me
as . . . that disgusting old man would have."

Nalin eyed Edge again at the sound of him
swallowing the food. And was in time to see
him shake his head before he answered:

"If there was any need to thank me, it'd be

just for bringing you with me. The rest of it wouldn't have applied if I hadn't done that."

Now she shook her head to deny what he was saying. Said vehemently as she continued to look at him: "I was a fool. I did not know how badly I was injured when I told you I wanted to remain with my dead people. Perhaps to die from being shot. Or to be killed by some other white man who found me—who was more like the boatman than you." She shrugged with just one shoulder, favoring her left side and not wincing. "Perhaps to be found and protected by the braves on their return. If they have not had trouble with the white eyes and do return. And if they think it worth their while to be burdened with one squaw who many do not look upon as true Arapaho."

"Yellow Shirt and his band are looking for trouble, Nalin?" Edge asked.

And the girl was mildly irritated to be sidetracked off the line she had taken so long to start out on. But this lasted just a moment and she spoke with feeling when she replied: "It was not meant to be so, Edge. When our land was taken from us by force, the elders say to the sub-chiefs that they should try to live on the reservation as the soldiers tell them. But the land was not good for our ways. Every Arapaho knows of this, but few have the will to escape what is little more than a prison for those whose only crime is to be Indian."

She glanced at Edge again, and saw that he was eating, still without enthusiasm for the food. And suspected, with a grimace, that he also lacked interest in the root problems of her people.

"You asked me," she said accusingly.

"I know," he replied evenly.

She paused to collect her thoughts and drank some coffee while she did so. Then went on: "Yellow Shirt would have gone alone. But many wished to join him. Braves and squaws, some with their children, and elders. Like those who were murdered at the camp by the source of the river."

She peered long and hard into the heart of the fire beneath the cooking pot. Her face and frame in profile totally unmoving, as if she was holding her breath while she recalled the merciless slaughter. Until she was startled out of her private world of remembered horror, by Edge moving into her line of sight—to ladle food from the pot to the plate, which he handed to her.

"Thank you," she said.

"You're welcome. Watch it, it's hot."

"There were too many followers of Yellow Shirt. This is a big country, but all the time more and more people—white eyes—come to claim it and build on it and fence it. We did not seek trouble. But white eyes who see so many Indians are frightened into making trouble for us. They fire their guns before they talk. And we Arapaho are a proud nation, Edge. We must meet force with force. But all the time we lose more people until Yellow Shirt has just thirty warrior braves and those of us he leaves at the camp beside the source of the river."

There was a deep sadness on her face and in her voice as she shook her head slowly and defended: "We came looking for a part of this land where we might live as our people before us lived. We did not want to fight the white eyes to get this, but they forced us to fight them. And now it is said in many places along the ways we have come that Yellow Shirt and his band of Arapaho are renegades, thieves and murderers of innocent white eyes." She sighed and gazed levelly at the half-breed. "So the answer, in truth, is no to your question. Yellow Shirt does not look for trouble, but in looking for what he seeks for those who follow him he is certain he will find it." Then a wan smile paid a brief visit to her beautiful young face as she spooned up a piece of meat and admitted: "Which wasn't at all what I started out to tell you, Edge. But it was you who asked about Yellow Shirt. Perhaps because you think it unmanly to talk of what I had it in mind to say?"

She spooned the meat into her mouth and chewed on it with obvious enjoyment—but whether she was relishing the taste of the food or the feeling that she had scored another point against the man, it was impossible to tell.

"Not that, girl," he said, a little brusquely. "When I know there's a bunch of Indians in the country I'm crossing, I also like to know whether or not they're hostile."

She considered this for a few moments, until

she had swallowed the first mouthful of food. Then she nodded and allowed, still pensive: "Yes, I can understand that." She continued eating, but abruptly had a thought that spread a frown across her face and injected a hardness into her tone. And she accused: "You bastard son of a bitch white eyes pig! You are not doing any of this to help me! It is all for yourself! You have brought me with you so that you may bargain for your life should my people threaten it! Is that not so, white eyes?"

"I don't recall I ever claimed I was—"

"That is just it!" the Arapaho girl cut in, so angry she forgot about her wound and the plate of food. Grimaced as she swung too fast to face him but then ignored the stab of pain in the same way as she paid no attention to the fact that the food had slid off the tilting plate. "You say hardly anything at all! You let me think what I do and make a fool of myself out of gratitude! And all the time I have nothing to be grateful to you for! Because you do what you do for selfish reasons!"

The silence that followed her diatribe was on this occasion obviously bothersome to the girl while the man appeared totally at his ease as he took the makings from his pocket and began to slowly roll a cigarette.

"You have nothing to say?" she demanded finally.

"I'm not looking for an argument," he replied evenly.

"Because you know what I say is true?"

"Only lie I ever accused you of was the one when you said you wanted to die, Nalin."

He rolled the tobacco in the paper, licked the paper, smoothed the join and hung the cigarette at the side of his mouth. This time he used a length of wood, alight at one end, to fire the cigarette. While the Arapaho girl stared fiercely at him, her mind racing to find some form of words that would stir him out of his apparent indifference to her opinion of him. But she failed, and could manage only to taunt:

"Damn you for being always right!"

"Nobody's that perfect."

"True, white eyes," she retorted and a glint of triumph entered her dark eyes. "If you knew you were that, you would have trusted yourself to attend to my wound—certain that to see and caress such an intimate part of my body would not inflame your lust!"

Edge said: "You want more to eat?"

"Yes, yes I do," she answered quickly, enjoying her victory. And took care to favor her injured side as she moved to replace from the cooking pot the food that had slid off her plate. Then continued to be tacitly content while she finished the meal and the half-breed drank more coffee—afterwards as he cleaned the dirty dishes and she stretched out in the single blanket but close enough to the fire to be kept warm by it. But he sensed a change in her attitude while he stoked the fire with fresh fuel so that it would burn for several hours. Felt that her dark eyes, expressing something close to pathos, followed his every move until he bedded down on the other side of the steadily burning fire. When, through the flickering flames and shimmering smoke, she called softly: "Edge?"

"Yeah?"

"I have benefited from your selfishness. So if we should meet with Yellow Shirt and you are in danger, I will do what I can to help you."

"It's a shame you're an Indian, Nalin," the half-breed replied.

"Why is that? You would treat me differently if I were of your race?"

"I'd be able to say that's real white of you, girl."

Chapter Six

WHETHER HE bedded down in open country on the ground or at a city hotel in a bed, Edge always slept with either his rifle or revolver close at hand. And at times when he felt particularly threatened he shared his bedding with a gun. Tonight in the ravine with the trees on one side and the bluff on the other, he slept with his right hand fisted around the Winchester that he kept pressed against his side. The rifle entirely hidden and his frame draped from chest to ankles by the sheepskin coat spread sideways over him—this after he had covered the Arapaho girl with a second blanket when she was deeply asleep and did not stir nor murmur at his approach and while he ensured she would be warm throughout the night.

Nalin, mentally and physically weary from the anguish and pain-filled day, took just a few minutes to sink into such a sound sleep. And, back under the sheepskin with his head resting

on his saddle, the half-breed was just as effort-
lessly quick to get to sleep. But he was far from
being exhausted in mind or body and the level
of unconsciousness into which he drifted was
much shallower.

It was natural for him to sleep this way at
times such as this. In a kind of doze, just short
of being awake, that was refreshing and restor-
ative while some animal-like sense of self-pres-
ervation remained alert. Ready to warn him of
danger nearby, so that he could come awake
from such a light sleep with total recall of his
situation and instant readiness to respond to
whatever had changed. Like so many other
aspects of this man's character and ability, this
way in which he slept had been developed during the long ago war. When it had been the
gray uniformed soldiers of the Confederate
army he needed to be on his guard against
when awake or asleep. And when the war was
over, the continual uncertainties of Edge's violent peace had led to the honing of such hard-
learned skills taught by such harsh conditions.
And on numerous occasions it had been hostile
Indians who posed the threat to the sleeping
man. Who more than once would have died had
he not slept so lightly, or come instantly awake
in full command of his responses to the menace.

Tonight when he was roused abruptly to
awareness of an alien presence, there was an
immediate visual image to confirm the warning
which was triggered by the inexplicable sense.
Of a man astride a horse, both unmoving, seen
in dark silhouette against the star-pricked and

moon-lightened sky. But, Edge knew, this was
not the only stranger nearby. And, main-
taining the same rate of breathing as while he
slept, he shifted only his eyes between their
cracked open lids as he searched for the rider's
companions.

The camp was much closer to the pines than
to the face of the bluff some three hundred feet
away. The Arapaho girl was bedded down on
the fringe of brush at the foot of the trees to
one side of the fire that had by now burned
down to a heap of powdery gray ash and glowing wood embers. Edge was stretched out on
the grass and his saddle under the sheepskin
coat on the directly opposite side of the fire, between it and the buckboard to the rear of which
the mules were hitched on long lines.

He could hear the animals as they breathed,
undoubtedly aware of strange horses and men
close by but not in the least disturbed by this.
He could not see the mules, though, nor any
other features of the ravine between the camp
and the river some half mile away. For he had
bedded down with his feet toward the southern
end of the ravine and without shifting his head
on the pillow of his saddle his view was restrict-
ed to the top of the rise where the immobile
man sat on his unmoving horse, the trees and
the bluff to either side and the open ground
within these confines.

The breathing of the mules, the softer sounds
made by the sleeping girl and the intake and
exhalation as he breathed—this loudest of all
to his own ears—were the only intrusions into

an otherwise total silence. This as Edge,
having recognized the man astride the horse as
an Indian brave, still failed to see or hear signs
of the others he was certain were very close.
Closer, probably, than the lone rider halted between the trees and the end of the bluff on the
crest of the high ground some five hundred feet
distant. Who presented such an easy target for
the man with the Winchester under the sheepskin coat. But who would not have moved into
so exposed a position unless he felt safe from a
surprise panic shot.

For perhaps a half minute the scene before
the half-breed and the sounds that went with it
remained unchanged. And it would be easy for
him to think that during this period only his
cracked open eyes and the smoke from the subdued fire, his own chest and that of the Indian,
the rider's eyes and the eyes and chest of the
horse moved. But it was seldom that the mind
of the man called Edge concerned itself with in-
consequentials. And in those thirty or so
seconds, it was unnecessary for him to make
any conscious effort to keep his mind a blank.

Then the Indian on the horse at the crest of
the rise thrust a clenched fist into the night
sky. And Edge became abruptly as taut as a
drum skin, but without even a stray wisp of
pre-conceived half thought entering his mind.
Until a bullet plunged into the center of the fire
with a minor explosion of ash and sparks. At
the same instant as the crack of the rifle was
heard, a moment before the girl awoke with a
choked cry of fear. Only then did Edge allow

himself to guess that he was not going to be killed immediately—unless he did something to panic the Indians. Because the single shots had hit the target it was aimed at, he knew. Fired by a brave regarded as the most skilled with a rifle. If his sudden death had been the intention, his body and not the fire would have taken the bullet. Or, the man on the horse would not have shown himself and a whole hail of gunfire would have poured down on the camp in the ravine.

"Nalin!" Edge rasped against the echo of the shot, her cry and the sounds of fear made by the mules.

"What is the—" she started to ask in a rasping whisper.

"Do something stupid and you could get to die among your own people," he replied flatly. "Feller on the pony to the south is somebody you know, I figure?"

The soft spoken words in the exchange served a secondary purpose—calmed the mules from their snorting, scraping at the ground and jerking on the hitching lines. There was a sound of utter silence and then the Arapaho girl vented another sound of shock.

"If you know him, tell him hello," Edge instructed, and there was a trace of tension in his voice now.

Nalin shouted something in her own language, apparently made a false start and began again. Warmed quickly to the subject and rose to her feet. She grimaced in response to the discomfort she felt but did not allow the

pain to be heard in her voice as she continued
to direct the fast-spoken stream of Arapaho
words up the rise toward the mounted brave.
She as unmoving as he after she had gained her
feet, both hands clutching the blanket to her
throat so not gesturing.

While Edge remained equally still under the
coat, right hand sweating a little where it was
fisted to the Winchester. And left hand taut to
streak up and out from hiding—to grasp the
gunbelt with its holstered Colt that was hooked over the horn of his saddle to the left of his
head. This as part of the same move that pow-
ered him into a roll—between the offside wheels
of the buckboard and into the insubstantial
cover of the neglected rig. From where he was
confident he could blast the brave on the horse.
And maybe trigger shots into a few more Indians before the inevitable happened and his
time was up.

But, if nothing in life is inevitable except for
death, the timing of the end always remains a
mystery. And Edge waited with easy equan-
imity for the solution, which in this instance,
depended upon the responses of the brave
astride the pony to whatever the squaw beside
the fire was saying to him.

Nalin addressed the brave for perhaps a full
minute while Edge watched the only intruder
in sight and listened for sounds that others
were closing in. When she was through, a
silence fell and its duration was stretched in
imagination by high tension. This ended when
the mounted brave spoke fast and briefly to the

girl, then shifted his attention to the top of the bluff that formed the western wall of the ravine. And spoke for longer, with less urgency.

"It will be all right, I think," Nalin whispered tensely to Edge as he kept his narrow-eyed gaze fixed on the rim of the ravine. "I have told Yellow Shirt you are friend of the Arapaho."

"And he told you?" Edge asked as a dozen or so braves moved forward to be skylined on the high ground. Each with a rifle in one hand and leading a pony by the reins with the other. Then the thud of unshod hooves drew the half-breed's attention back to the southern end of the ravine. In time to see Yellow Shirt start his mount down the slope, followed by a group of other braves astride ponies.

"That if you wish to die, you will know what to do. I think it unnecessary to tell you this, unless you ask."

The braves on the rim of the ravine swung up astride their ponies and began to file forward to join the group led by the chief. As Edge released his grip on the Winchester, eased both his hands slowly out from under the coat and came cautiously to his feet.

"I have told of the killings at the camp beside the source of the river," Nalin said, her nervousness increasing as the large band of rifle toting Indians came closer. "Yellow Shirt's wife and baby son and his parents are among the dead. So his temper will not be good toward a white eyes."

"I can understand that," Edge answered as

he stooped to pick up his hat and the sheepskin
coat. And put them on, the sweat suddenly
cold against his flesh, as Yellow Shirt rasped
another burst of harshly spoken words toward
the girl. Who waited in a servile attitude for the
chief to finish and allowed time to pass to be
sure he was through before she replied in a tone
of voice that was as subservient as her manner.

The Arapaho band had ridden close enough
now to be seen clearly in the moonlight that
reached to the bottom of the ravine. About
thirty of them, spanning in age from a boy of
eighteen or so to an upper limit of perhaps
forty five. A morose and grim-faced bunch of
braves as they experienced the shock of learn-
ing about the massacre of the elders, squaws
and children. All of them ill dressed for the
coldness of this pre-winter night in fabric leggings, breechcloths and shirts of waistcoats.
All with feathered headbands but few with any
other form of ornamentation. There were probably more who were bare foot than there were
who wore moccasins.

The chief was one of the few who had a revolver on his weapons belt along with a knife
and tomahawk. And he also had a saddle on his
pony, with a boot into which his rifle was
lodged. All the others had straps on their rifles
so that the guns could be carried across their
backs.

Just before Yellow Shirt made a hand gesture to halt the party, Nalin told Edge: "I am
the only Arapaho here who speaks your lan-

guage. But take care. Many will understand what you say."

Then the newcomers stopped their advance, some twenty feet away, with Yellow Shirt slightly ahead of the rest. Empty handed while they all sat their ponies with the stocks of their rifles resting on their thighs and the muzzles aimed at the night sky. Here and there a single shot model, but mostly repeaters. All of the weapons quite old.

Every pair of dark eyes in unmoving faces directed a hostile glower toward Edge, until Yellow Shirt alone looked away from him to speak to Nalin. To ask, in a voice that became less harsh as time past, a series of apparently straightforward questions to which the girl gave concise and unhesitating responses. Sometimes, one of her answers would cause a brave or a group of them to scowl or frown or even wince. But the countenance of the chief never altered from its impassiveness that was a match for the look on the lean face of Edge.

Yellow Shirt was of an age with the half-breed, too. But in appearance, they had nothing else in common. The Arapaho was a head shorter and his frame was stocky rather than spare. His hair was more gray than black and worn shorter. While his face was round with slightly squashed features to create a look that was neither handsome nor ugly but was somehow commanding.

He did not shift his dark eyes back to Edge until the full horror of the massacre had been

drawn from the girl. Then Yellow Shirt looked
long and hard at the half-breed, the rifle at his
feet where he had bedded down, the saddle
which had been his pillow and the gunbelt
hooked over the saddle horn. And, after this
five second survey, spoke in a questioning
tone. There was a pause, then a snarling rebuke
for Nalin accompanied by a scornful glance.

The girl appeared to apologize to the leader
of the Indians and quickly translated for Edge:
"Chief Yellow Shirt asks me to tell you he
compliments you on not trying to make use of
your weapons after the warning shot was
fired."

The half-breed continued to hold the level
gaze of the Arapaho chief while the girl spoke.
Now nodded briefly and answered: "Tell him I
appreciate getting the warning. Better in the
heart of the fire than mine."

Nalin did the reverse translation and Yellow
Shirt nodded. Then hardened his expression
and voice to speak again to Edge. Speaking a
sentiment with which his braves agreed—all of
them equally as determined as the chief as they
nodded their endorsement of his words, sat
more rigidly in their saddles and took a firmer
grip around the frames of their rifles. While
this was happening, the girl's beautiful face
with the single blemish of the scar on the jaw
showed an expression that was a mixture of
anxiety and sadness. And she listened intently
to Yellow Shirt, to make certain of when he was
through so that he could not bawl her out
again for being laggard with the translation.

"Chief Yellow Shirt asks me to tell you, Edge," she said quickly, "that neither you nor any other white eyes will ever again be dealt with so mercifully as this. We go now, to bury our dead according to the Arapaho custom. And when the burial is complete, Chief Yellow Shirt will take his braves on the warpath. Until the white eyes who killed our people are themselves killed. You are told this so that you may leave this part of the country with all speed. In return for the care you have taken of me. Even though I am more than ever unworthy as an Arapaho squaw for asking help of a white eyes."

Now the power of her gaze was suddenly stronger than that of the chief and Edge felt drawn to shift his attention to Nalin. To read in her lovely face a tacit but forceful plea that he should not take issue with what she said—either her lie to Yellow Shirt or the way in which she faithfully reported his low opinion of her.

"Tell him it was no sweat," he replied. "And that I'm the last feller to stand in the way of somebody doing what they want, unless—"

He broke off what he was saying as the Arapaho chief uttered a sound of impatience and heeled his pony forward—jerked on the rope reins to steer the animal toward where the slight-figured, beautiful-faced and abruptly very frightened girl stood.

"It's all right!" she snapped at Edge as she sensed the sudden upsurge of tension in the atmosphere of the camp site.

Many of the braves sensed the same change,
that seemed for stretched seconds to heat up
the chill air of the night. And at least a dozen
rifles were shifted from where they rested and
came to bear on the single target of the sheepskin-coated, Stetson-hatted man standing between the almost dead fire and the near derelict
buckboard. But Edge did no more than direct
his ice cold, slit-eyed gaze at Yellow Shirt and
draw back his lips fractionally to expose his
teeth in a silent snarl.

And then the chief halted his mount and extended a hand at a position and in a gesture
that invited the girl to share his pony. And,
with a soft spoken word that was probably of
gratitude, Nalin clasped his hand with one of
her own, placed a foot in the stirrup he freed for
her and swung up to sit on the cantle behind
him. The agony this caused her was clear to see
—showed in a grimace that came close to turning her beauty into ugliness. But she was able
to hide this from Yellow Shirt and the braves
by hanging her head. And if any of the Arapaho heard the soft cry of pain she vented, they
ignored it. Perhaps for Nalin's benefit.

Then the chief replaced his foot in the stirrup
and spoke tense words to Edge as all the
braves' rifles once more were shifted to cant
their barrels at the sky.

"Unless what he wants and what I want is
the same thing," Edge concluded.

"Chief Yellow Shirt asks me to tell you good-
bye, white eyes," Nalin translated, with a
glower in response to what the half-breed had

said, as the pony with two riders started along the ravine toward the river. And the rest of the braves urged their mounts forward—following the same line between the almost dead fire and the band of timber. Only the most suspicious, or the Arapaho who were more deeply affected by news of the massacre, directed hatred filled stares at the white man they would patently rather not have left alive.

But none of them looked back over their shoulders once they had ridden away from the campsite. And Edge ignored the large band of Indians as he squatted by the fire and used an unburnt length of tree branch to stir the flames from the ashes. Then put a pot of coffee on the fire and rolled and smoked a cigarette as he waited for it to boil—and dawn stretched dirty fingers of half light into the night sky. By which time the Arapaho were gone from the ravine and perhaps had even crossed the river. Certainly they were nowhere to be seen when, his gunbelt slung around his waist and the rifle canted to his shoulder, he ambled down to the river. Which was two mugs of coffee later. There, at the inlet, he washed up and shaved in the cold water under the unwarm rays of the rising sun, and refilled his canteens. While all that moved within his sight on the north side of the slow flowing river were a half dozen buzzards, scavanging those portions of the Frenchman's body and the gelding's carcass that had been shunned by the coyotes.

Back at the night camp he drank a third mug of coffee and then doused the fire, put the

animals in the traces and loaded the buckboard
with his few possessions—including the one
blanket that Nalin had left on the ground when
she swung astride Yellow Shirt's mount. More
than an hour ago, so that whatever warmth it
felt of was from the weak sun rather than her
youthful body. And it smelled only of its
owner's old sweat, the smoke of many camp-
fires and of a horse that was now dead.

Up on the seat, with the brake lever released,
he snapped the reins and ordered: "Okay you
mules, take off. This ain't no time to think
about putting my feet up."

Chapter Seven

IT WAS mid-afternoon when Edge saw a smudge of smoke against a distant horizon again. Far to the south east across the prairie-like plain that had few prominant features until the ground began to rise with the foothills of the rugged mountains that had never appeared to be any closer to the buckboard since he had driven it out of the ravine an hour after dawn.

But there was no omen of trouble in the smoke this time as he saw that its source did not remain in one place and that the cloud it formed was elongated. And guessed that it was streaming from the stack of a locomotive, heading from the east into the west along a track that, unless it curved, would intersect with the trail he was on some ten miles or so due south. In the vicinity of an extensive mesa which was the only outcrop of rock of any size between the river and the mountain range. A towering, three-sided mass of sandstone that the trapper

who had told Edge about it said was called Trio
Bluff. Under the south west facing side of
which was the town of Calendar, Territory of
New Mexico. The old trapper had made no
mention of a railroad passing through town,
but he did say it was more than seven years
since he was last through there himself.

Much more recent callers, if the tracks on the
dusty trail ran all the way into Calendar, were
the two men who had committed the carnage at
the Arapaho encampment. Since getting onto
the trail stretching between the ferry and the
town, Edge had paid no particular attention to
the sign left by the wagon and horses of the
murdering Indian traders. Except to note that
the hoof and wheel tracks were the freshest on
the trail surface by several days. Which perhaps, accounted, he had mused indifferently
while driving across the vast flatland, for the
run down condition of the ferryman, his house,
his raft and his wagon. Because so few passengers came by to use his river crossing any
more and money was therefore short. Maybe
the railroad ultimately and more rapidly reached the same destination as the trail, the half-
breed reflected as he saw the moving cloud of
smoke make for Trio Bluff and the freight and
the passengers that had once needed the ferry
of Maziol now made use of the train.

It was not only money the Frenchman was
no longer getting, Edge allowed as the last
traces of cordwood smoke disappeared in the
afternoon air when the locomotive and cars
were beyond one of the bluff's three corners, to

explain his improvised state. He also lacked the human contact of more prosperous days—and was not the first man the half-breed had met at an isolated frontier outpost who had been driven crazy by loneliness.

Abruptly, Edge spoke an obscenity, spat over the side of the seat and dug out the makings to roll a cigarette. Was totally ignored by the pair of mules which plodded along the arrow straight trail at the same pace as they always had done—would stop and start immediately to the dictates of the man with the reins but move only at the single speed they chose. Which was slow and energy conserving and suited Edge.

What did not suit him was this unbidden line of thought from indifferent reflections upon the material conditions surrounding the Frenchman to his state of mental health and a possible reason for it. Because that struck too close to where Edge was living at present and there was a danger he would, involuntarily again, start to draw parallels to try to explain his own feelings to himself.

So he took deliberate pains with the making and smoking of the cigarette. And paid far closer attention than was necessary to his surroundings. Next made a careful check of both the Frontier Colt and the Winchester, like he expected to have to use the guns soon. Which was always a strong possibility. But there was certainly no immediate danger, for the terrain was such that until night fell he was able to gaze over a distance of many miles in every direction and saw no sign of any threat. But, by indulging in such mild physical activity and consciously considering what he was doing, he was able to bar the unwelcome thought process from his mind.

Then night came and, as always, the troubled mind was more vulnerable to further attack in the encapsulating darkness when the alone are never more lonely . . .

Abruptly again, Edge uttered another obscenity. But in a snarling tone of self anger this time, that caused the mules to prick their ears. But the animals immediately became easy again when no further sound was vented by their driver and no command was given through the reins. For if, as many animals are thought to, these were able to sense the mood of the man in charge of them, they elected with the stubbornness of their kind to ignore it. Obstinately content to go their own way in their own fashion until an outside influence made demands on them—when they were more likely to want to do the opposite of what was pressed upon them . . . .

Edge, his anger subdued only moments after the accusation of being lonely sparked it, now remained coldly calm as he checked this new unwelcome musing that would have him consider himself not only as crazy as the French ferryman but also as unreasonably obdurate as a mule!

Then he showed a brief half grin that bared the tops of his teeth but failed to inject warmth into the glittering slits of his eyes as he murmured: "Well, maybe you fellers and me have something in common. Maybe all half-breeds are stubborn bastards, you figure?"

The pair of mules did not even prick their ears at the sound of his soft spoken words as they hauled the buckboard around the north east corner of Trio Bluff and started along the final stretch of trail into Calendar. And Edge was able to keep his mind free of disturbing thoughts as he looked toward the town that was seen in ever increasing detail as he closed with it.

The trail was running in a south west direction now, staying close to the base of the more than a mile long and one hundred and fifty feet high wall of weather-eroded sandstone. Beyond the southern tip of the wedge-shaped mesa the trail continued in the same direction, alongside the single track of the railroad that curved to avoid Trio Bluff and paralleled the trail for three-quarters of a mile or so until the single street of town had its start at the train station. Halfway between the mesa's southern tip and the depot there was a plank crossing of the trail over the railroad and a switchgear where another track swung away from the Calendar spur to head out to the west.

The train that Edge had seen approaching from the east in the afternoon was still at the station. Comprised of an eight-wheeled locomotive with a high stack and a cowcatcher, its tender, three day cars, a sleeper and a caboose. The engine was silent and no smoke rose from its stack nor steam hissed from its valves. And

all the cars were darkened—looked as deserted
as the depot platform did for most of its length.
Also in darkness was the steeply pitched roof-
ed, many gabled, frame-constructed station
building sited midway along the platform. But
a number of lamps were alight in the vicinity of
the locomotive and its cabin was also well lit.
While two men worked on the engine and more
stood grouped on the platform beside it.

Once he had gone over the crossing and rolled the buckboard by the caboose, Edge was on
the blind side of the train from the platform
and able to look down the length of Calendar's
only street beyond the sand-filled box that
served as a substantial buffer at the end of the
railroad track. A street that was a half mile or
so in length and flanked by buildings which
with a few exceptions were single story, of
timber and a good deal older than the station.
The usual stores and other commercial prem-
ises for business or pleasure, a church and a
school, a meeting hall and a law office. While as
new as the depot building was the Railroad
Hotel which had a frame second story above a
stone first, a row of four small houses and the
Restawhile Restaurant. These at the north end
of the street. While at the southern end there
was an area of stockyards and attendant buildings of recent construction.

With the exception of the deserted section
down at the stockyards, the town was well
enough lit to negate the effect of the moon and
stars and the broad, unsidewalked street was

quietly lively with people. But only one other wagon moved on it. Emerged from an alley between two buildings close to the southern end and turned to come northward. A solid topped freight wagon with shiny paintwork and ornately lettered signs on the side panels, drawn by a team of four horses. With the driver and another man up on the high seat, both of them city-suited, neck-tied and Derby-hatted. The passenger holding a cone-shaped object in both hands, the wider end resting on his thighs.

The wagon was driven up the right side of the street for most of its length, then angled across toward the front of the hotel which was on the left side. And, as Edge drove the buckboard past the locomotive of the stalled train, he was able to glimpse the lettering on one side of the freight wagon, painted gold blocked blue on bright red:

N	WE SELL EVERYTHING	N
O		O
T	MARX & SPENSER	V
I		E
O	VALUE & QUALITY	L
N		T
S	GUARANTEED	I
		E
&		S

On the footplate of the locomotive, a man with a strong Irish accent exclaimed: "Holy saints, Michael, will you look at that!"

"So it's the chain stored up trouble for old

number five-oh-one, Sean!" another Irishman
answered.

"Can you fix it?" a harassed and impatient
man with no pronounced accent called from the
platform.

"Looks to have been the wrong size when it
was new, sir," Sean answered. "Reckon we'd
best change it."

"Do it then!"

"Surely, sir."

The buckboard with the stranger driving it
was beyond the out-of-commission locomotive
now. And in a railroad town where strangers
were a regular occurence he was spared no
more than a cursory glance by the railroadmen
at the depot. Who had no time to offer a greet-
ing. While, with a few exceptions, the people on
the street who were converging into a group at
the traders' wagon were equally indifferent to
his arrival at Calendar. Townspeople and temp-
orarily stranded train passengers alike, who
probably would have failed to give him a
second glance even if their attention were not
in process of being captured by the freight
wagon.

A man with a peace officer's badge pinned to
the left pocket of his shirt kept a cautious eye
on Edge as he steered the buckboard carefully
around the rear of the throng gathered at the
freight wagon parked out front of the hotel. A
much older man with an unshaven face, almost
no teeth and no hair at all divided his distrust-
ful attention between the buckboard and its
driver. While less overt in their slightly

nervous interest—but clearly seen by the narrowed, ice blue eyes of the half-breed—were the
two men who were the big attraction in town
this clear, chill evening.

"Thank you, thank you, thank you, fine
people of this fine little town and you folks who
have been forced to stopover here in Calendar
while the train engine is repaired! And let me
tell you right now, you'll all be thanking me
and my partner before very long! And those of
you off the train who've been a little peeved by
the delay, you'll have reason to rejoice!"

It was the man who rode as passenger on the
freight wagon who made the enthusiastic announcement, standing up on the seat and using
the tin megaphone to amplify his voice, swinging it from left to right so that his words
carried to every part of the small town. And he
seemed now to be ignoring Edge as his partner
started to climb down from the wagon, smiling
nervously as he requested the pressing crowd
to ease back while he shot occasional glances
over their heads toward the newly arrived
buckboard.

"I'm Eddie Marx, folks!" the spokesman for
the drummers went on. "And the gent stepping
down to show you our wares is Jason Spenser!
And like it says right there on the sides of our
vehicle, we sell everything and we guarantee
everything we sell! But we just have the one
vehicle—at present—and so Jason and I have
to restrict the range of merchandise we bring
out on the road with us. . . ."

Marx went on with his spiel, expertly holding

the interest of the crowd he already had while the less quick to respond now started along the street to swell his audience. Glibly delivering a speech he had obviously spouted many times before, but in such a way that it seemed to sound as fresh to himself as to the citizens and enforced visitors to Calendar.

He was about thirty. Not five and a half feet tall and stockily built so that he looked to have a strong physique. He had blond hair that was neatly clipped and he was clean shaven, his round and chubby face red and shiny from where he had recently washed up. His clothing was also neat and clean, conservative in style and colors to contrast with the garishly painted wagon.

Spenser was ten years older. Six feet tall and broadly built, with pudgy hands and a flabby face that suggested that equally well cut business suit was hung on a large frame that owed more to excess fat than to muscular development. He had brown hair and a thick mustache of the same hue that did not droop at each side of his full-lipped mouth. His eyes were brown and as soft looking as the rest of his appearance—so that even when he smiled he seemed to harbor sadness in back of the expression. He wore an expensive looking jeweled ring on the third finger of each hand and a pearl headed stickpin in his necktie. The first and second finger of his left hand were darkly stained from holding countless cigars or cigarettes. Perhaps he was naturally clumsy, or maybe it was his nervousness at seeing Edge that caused him to be so awkward in removing the side and rear panels of the wagon, the half-breed reflected as the mules came to a halt of their own accord outside of the Cottonwood Saloon, diagonally across the street from the hotel.

"Evenin' to you, stranger," the man leaning against the wall to one side of the saloon's bat-winged entrance greeted, speaking around the live match that angled from a corner of his mouth. He was the man with the badge. Anything from fifty to sixty years old, with a burnished and deeply lined face and a broad-shouldered, narrow-waisted and slender-hipped build. Gray haired and dark eyed. In need of a shave and wearing Western style clothing that had seen better days and probably would have to endure some worse ones before he considered changing for new. He was the only other man on the street who carried a gun that showed—a Smith and Wesson .44 caliber Russian with a barrel longer than the usual six and a half inches. Slid into a tied down holster on the right side of his gunbelt—the toe of the holster cut to allow the extra length barrel to protrude.

"Evening," Edge replied, like the lawman speaking against the constant barrage of selling words that Marx was spreading over his audience. But the drummer had abandoned the megaphone now that he was sure the crowd was as big as he was going to get.

"Cy Meek," the lawman said with a curt nod, continuing to suck on the match and to lean against the wall of the saloon.

"Edge," the half-breed countered, staying aboard the Frenchman's wagon, but turning on the seat to look over the heads of the crowd across the street, into the interior of the freight wagon that was now exposed by the removal of the panels.

"I'm the sheriff of this town," Meek said, and there was a tone of irritation in his voice as he spoke to the stranger whose attention he had apparently lost.

"I'm just somebody passing through, sheriff," came the even voiced reply. "Figure to head on out after I've purchased some supplies."

The glinting blue eyes of the half-breed were briefly distracted from the display of merchandise on the wagon across the street. And he met, for just a moment, the gaze directed at him by the baldheaded and almost toothless old timer who was watching him from the dimly lit open doorway beside the blacked out window of Cecil Downing's Undertaking Parlor midway along the western side of the street. The old man, attired in somber clothing in more urgent need of renewal than the outfit of the sheriff, was looking at the half-breed in a way he had become used to being surveyed by strangers who perceived him to be a drifting loner unlike most others of his type. And so he returned his attention to the uncovered freight wagon, aware that the lawman had seen the distant exchange of anxious resentment for disdainful indifference.

"Name that matches my nature, most of the

time, Mr. Edge," Meek said. "Along with mild."

"Like my name, sheriff, I can sometimes be real sharp, sheriff. Right now though, I'm going to be blunt."

"About them two drummers?" Meek was both interested and wary, as if he felt he should hear what the stranger had to say but knew he would not like it.

"Hey, you fellers with the Indian stuff to sell!" Edge yelled, his voice cutting across and curtailing the excitedly spoken sales talk of Marx. And abruptly the half-breed was the focal point of all attention. Work even halted on the broken down locomotive as the railroadmen became conscious of a tension in the sudden silence that dropped over the town. A silence during which Edge was disconcertingly aware of breaking one of the few rules by which he lived his life, and momentarily regretted it before he went on—speaking to forestall an attack by a different brand of embarrassment to that he had unfamiliarly endured when he was with Nalin. "If any of it has blood on it, is the price higher?"

Spenser looked toward Marx with a plea emanating from every line of his face. While Marx switched his expression from a glower to a grin as he held the ice-eyed gaze of Edge and yelled back:

"Depends, mister! If Jason or I can guarantee the blood's genuine, then it makes the item more expensive! But if we bought the item off an Indian who might well have stained it with

animal blood, then we make no extra charge!
Does that answer your question, sir?"

"Hey, you got any artifacts that you can
guarantee have real blood of a real Indian on
them, Mr. Marx?" a matronly looking blond-
haired woman in the crowd asked excitedly.

"I'd sure like to see some!" a man added with
similar eagerness. "My wife back home in Caro-
lina would just love to have an Apache moc-
casin or somethin' like that with the blood of
the savage that wore it still—"

"You don't want old style stuff like that,"
the half-breed cut in on the souvenir hunter.
"Latest fashion is Arapaho artifacts. Right,
drummer?"

Marx had not allowed the grin to slip from
his ruddy-complexioned face. And now he
broadened the expression and nodded vigorously as he divided his attention between his
audience, Edge and the wares displayed on the
wagon. While he returned to his sales pitch.

"The gentleman is absolutely correct, folks!
Why, it sounds almost as if he is a partner of
Jason Spenser and myself! Is that not so,
Jason?"

The older, taller and more heavily built man
was less expert at concealing his true feelings.
And was broodingly uneasy as he constantly
chewed at his top lip beneath the thick mustache and switched his gaze back and forth between Marx and Edge. With eyes that continued to be vaguely sad. He did not respond to
the query and his garrulous partner hurried on

after just a fleeting half scowl to reveal he was angered by the lack of co-operation.

"A large number of the items you see arrayed before you were obtained from a band of Arapaho Indians! Feathers and moccasins, chokers and ties, breechclouts and aprons, shirts and leggings, armbands and anklets, folks. And we have a good range of bead jewelry! A drum or two as used by the Indians when performing war dances!"

While he listed the goods for sale, the drummer waved a hand to indicate the exposed rear of the wagon on which it was all displayed. Along with much that was not of Indian origin —jars of candy, pots and pans, cartons of stationery, some wooden toys, a number of books, bottles of scent and packages of powders, some medicines in a variety of containers, framed prints of seascapes and a number of stringed musical instruments.

Just once during this time, he was able to catch the eye of the obviously perturbed Spenser, when he gestured with hands and head that the man should play his part in emphasizing the artifacts being mentioned. But the scowling man remained where he stood beside a rear corner of the wagon, and just shook his head.

"Ain't you got no weapons, mister?" a man wanted to know in sour tones. "No knives or tomahawks or bows? With arrows to go with them, maybe?"

"I'm sorry, sir," Marx countered hurriedly.

"The party of Arapaho Jason Spenser and I
parlayed with to obtain this merchandise were
not of a warlike disposition. They—"

"Sheriff?" Edge said, looking and sounding
the same as when he had first intervened to
hinder the drummers. Remained on the seat of
the buckboard, half turned to look across the
street. No hint in his even tone and impassive
expression of the ice cold anger that was con-
centrated at the pit of his stomach—or the
effort he needed to make it keep it from expanding and becoming critically hot.

"Somethin' you should know, mister," the
lawman countered, his voice also lacking tension or volume. But it acted to hold the both
eager and anxious attention of the large crowd
across the street that had initially been captured by Edge in speaking the single word.

And now it was the half-breed's turn to become the focus of every eye again, as he ignored the implication of a warning from Meek
and said to the sheriff while he directed his
glinting-eyed gaze elsewhere:

"There are no Indian weapons aboard that
wagon because there were none to be had. Just
a whole arsenal of rifles these fellers used to
gun down the Indians so they could steal the
stuff."

Marx and Spenser exchanged a glance and
on this occasion both were equally uneasy. But
in back of the older man's nervousness was a
tacit question. To which his partner was about
to reply with a nod, until the potential

customer for Arapaho weapons put in, as sour
toned as ever:

"Well, good for them, Injun lover! A bunch
of redskin savages gettin' blasted away is the
best news I heard this year!"

Eddie Marx vented a silent sigh through
compressed lips, and then resurrected his
familiar grin—with a glint of triumph added—
when a woman in the crowd rasped:

"So now you had some good news, Otis Snyder, maybe you'll stop being the biggest misery
in town. Some hope!"

There were a few gusts of high humored
laughter, and some nervous titters. And the
blond-haired, chubby-faced, stockily-built
Marx prepared to strike while the mood was
there and reopen his sales pitch. But a number
of people in his audience still remained turned
toward the half-breed, as if they were trapped
by some palpable force emanating from the ice
blue slivers of his eyes. And it was Edge who
spoke before the drummer could utter the first
word his lips shaped.

"Women, children and old men past the time
for carrying arms, sheriff. Counted four babies
not old enough to walk."

A stretched second of almost total silence followed the even-voiced revelation, kept from
being absolute by the shrill chirpings of many
cicadas. Then one of the repairmen working on
the locomotive dropped a tool that clattered
noisily on the footplate. And exclamations
ranging from horrified shock to brutal con-

tempt exploded in an odd sounding chorus
from the crowd. While frowns of every degree,
some sour scowls and several triumphant grins
showed on the faces of the people at the side of
the wagon.

This for another stretched second, before the
expressions became frozen and the chirping of
the cicadas provided the only sound in the
whole of Calendar again. The fresh shock again
signaled by Edge. But with actions instead of
words this time. The half-breed powering to his
feet and turning from the waist, as his right
hand streaked to the holstered Colt, fingers
curled and thumb extended. To grip the butt of
the revolver and cock the hammer as the barrel
slid clear of the holster. And the gun was tilted
up to become leveled from the hip, the forefinger across the trigger. All this performed as
part of a single, fluid movement that seemed to
take place in the batting of an eyelid. But not
one of the eyelids hooded over the glittering
slits of the half-breed's eyes, which did not
blink as he watched Jason Spenser. And saw
the drummer stoop, open a box slung under the
rear of the wagon and come upright with what
he had taken from the box. Did not himself
start to come erect and draw the Colt before he
saw the Winchester Spenser held in a two-
handed grip.

"No, Jase!" Eddie Marx roared, his complexion shaded from ruddy to near purple as his
voice reached almost feminine shrillness.

Marx was staring down at Spenser as he
shrieked the plea. And Edge was concentrating

his attention on both men. Which perhaps made them the only two people on the street who did not see how the sheriff of Calendar responded to the threat of gunplay in his town. But then, as Spenser thumbed back the hammer of the repeater while the rifle was still aimed at the night sky, the half-breed sensed danger behind him. And a part of a second later was aware that the source of that danger had captured a large share of tension-filled attention.

Jason Spenser was among those who felt compelled to look from Edge to Meek, and he was suddenly locked in a frozen attitude with the Winchester still not aimed at a target.

"Goin' to kill you sure as the Devil made little green applies to give folks the bellyache, Edge," the lawman said grimly. "If you fire your gun with intent to kill either or both them men over there. And after seein' how fast you are with that gun, I won't have no bad feelin' about back shootin' you."

The half-breed remained as immobile as Spenser while Meek spoke. But without the startled look that had spread suddenly over the fleshy face of the salesman. And now he moved just his lips to counterwarn the lawman:

"It's just as sure, sheriff, that I'm going to kill you. . . ." He paused briefly until the gasped and other subdued utterances of shock had died down. " . . . if you ever again aim a gun at me and don't kill me first. Same goes for everybody else who can hear me. Always try to give folks the warning. Just the once."

He needed to move his hand just fractionally back, to tilt the revolver and slide it into the holster. But kept his thumb on the cocked hammer and his forefinger to the trigger until Spenser obeyed Marx's hissed command to:

"Put the damn rifle down, Jase."

Then Edge eased the hammer of the Colt forward after Spenser had performed a similar action on the Winchester and dropped his hand away from the holstered gun after directing a cold-eyed glance over his shoulder to check that Meek was putting up his long-barreled Smith and Wesson. Then relief became a rasping sound that drowned out the chirping of the insects.

"That somethin' I was tellin' you, you oughta know about this town, Mr. Edge?" the sheriff said.

The half-breed turned all the way around and Eddie Marx at once began over again to capture the attention and imagination of this audience:

"Now folks, wasn't that kinda scary and exciting? Well, no more exciting than some of the items Jason Spenser is going to show you! And every last one of them genuine, if it's souvenirs of savage Indians that interests you! But that's not all we have to offer. Merchandise from all four corners of the. . . ."

Against the huckstering patter of the man aboard the freight wagon, Edge said wearily as he climbed down from the buckboard: "Yeah?"

"Calendar folks don't care much for Indians. Of any nation or any kind."

"Obliged, sheriff," the half-breed answered, as he dragged his gear off the rear of the buck-board to bundle it under his left arm.

Meek jerked a crooked thumb at the entrance of the saloon. "Buy you a drink?"

"Always pay my own way."

"Have it your way."

"Usually do, sheriff."

The lawman shrugged as he turned away to push open one of the batwing doors and say: "Well, I'm gonna have a brew myself. After you."

Edge shook his head to decline the offer of entering the Cottonwood Saloon in front of Sheriff Meek. And told him evenly: "Obliged again, but the way things are here, I'd rather not have the law behind me."

Chapter Eight

THE SALOON was longer than it was wide, stretching three times as much back from the street as its two story facade on the street. It was brightly lit by twin rows of ceiling hung kerosene lamps, but empty of patrons until the grim-faced sheriff and the impassive half-breed entered.

Two people were behind the long bar counter that stretched three-quarters of the way down the left side of the elongated room, beyond which was a dais on which stood a closed lid piano, three chairs and three music stands. A strip of uncluttered space, some ten feet wide, reached all the way from the front to the rear of the room. And on the other side of this was an array of close-packed, chair-ringed tables. Most of them bare topped but a few, in the far corner, covered with green baize for card games or with mechanical gambling equipment on them —two roulette wheels, boards for Diana and

Hazard, a wheel of fortune and the goose and jar of balls for Keno.

There were oil paintings on the walls, two mirrors behind the bar, sawdust on the floor and plain dust on most everything. The place smelled of kerosene oil rather than tobacco smoke, liquor and sweat.

The two men who were at the end of the bar closest to the window that gave a view out on the street looked like a father and son. The one close to fifty, fat and pale and balding and smilingly anxious to please. The other in his early twenties—slender in build and with a thin and callow face. A head taller than his father, showing no sign of ever having had to struggle with his conscience or work until he was ready to drop when the task finished. Resentful of the fact that he might have to be of service to the only customers in the place.

The older man rasped something out of the side of his mouth to the young one, who needed no further urging to withdraw to the far end of the bar counter where he leaned forward, head in his hands, to pore over a book.

"Mr. Meek, Mr. Edge," the older bartender greeted effusively. "I'm real glad that situation out there did not get ugly. And in celebration of this, I offer you a first drink on the house."

Both bartenders were dressed in white shirts, black bow ties, black pants and white waist aprons. The white parts of their outfits a little wilted looking and grubby. And the man who made the free drinks offer soiled his apron some more when he rubbed his sweaty palms down it, as his only two customers bellied up to the bar, Edge dropping his gear to the floor in front of it.

"Don't be stupid, Hans," Meek growled. "I know you can't afford to give liquor away and Mr. Edge always pays for what he has—as you well overheard if you caught his name."

The bartender shrugged his fleshy shoulders and made his smile wan as he pulled a foaming beer for the sheriff. Then said, as he drew another at a nod from the half-breed:

"But it sounds good, Mr. Meek. To say it. Even if I did hear what Mr. Edge told you. And know that even if you knew I could afford to give you a drink, you would not accept it. Because as sheriff of this town you want to owe nobody a favor."

"Sure, Hans," Meek said absently. "This here is Hans Linder, Mr. Edge. And down there is his son Bruno."

"From Germany, but now Americans, Mr. Edge," the older Linder said smilingly. "I am very pleased to know you."

"Figure customers'd be welcome here if you know them or not, feller?" the half-breed said after he had taken half the beer at a swallow. And now placed a dollar bill on the bar top alongside Meek's dime. "Bottle of whiskey and a shot glass, uh?"

"You bet." The order was filled and there were a few coins in change that Edge put in his pocket before he emptied the beer glass, left it on the bar counter and went with the shot glass and bottle to the nearest table. He also left his gear where it was.

"It will happen for us and when it does, we will be ready for it, sir!" Hans Linder said emphatically, and drew a sound of disdain from his scowling son.

"I ain't happy for you, feller," the half-breed said. "But don't mind me. Been a rough day."

The medium height, slenderly built, good-looking for his age Cy Meek turned from the bar with his glass held in both hands and leaned back comfortably, a heel hooked over the rail. And said: "Hans means about the herds and the drovers, Mr. Edge. Now we got the AT and SF spur down into Calendar, the ranchers down south will start comin' to our town."

Bruno Linder, without raising his eyes from the book, vented another inarticulate sound. That could have been taken to be a whole lot cruder than the first had the lawman been of a mind to treat it as such. But only the boy's father directed a frowning look toward him. While Meek continued to peer at Edge as the half-breed poured whiskey into the shot glass until it was brimful. The sheriff waiting for a response which was not delivered until the whiskey was downed in a single swallow and the glass refilled. When Edge began to roll a cigarette and asked:

"You got a reason for telling me this, I figure?"

Meek nodded. "If the Kansas cow towns are anythin' to go by, railheads can get to be pretty damn rough and tough places. Not our intention to have that happen here in Calendar. So we're takin' a hard line with troublemakers right from the start."

Outside, across the street, Eddie Marx had completed his sales talk and now the buying had begun. A lot of people were talking now, but with less forceful stridency. Occasionally, the sound of metal striking metal rang out from the disabled locomotive.

The half-breed struck a match on the butt of his Colt to light the cigarette, and said on a trickle of smoke: "Times ain't been so good for this town until now?"

He looked pointedly about himself—at the interior of the Cottonwood Saloon which in many ways typified the town of which it was a part. Once it had been less than half its present size, until an extension was built on at the rear—the enlarged whole now under-used by customers and neglected by the owner.

"They were good for us when we wanted only what we had, stranger," Bruno Linder said in an accent that was much thicker than his father's. Speaking with his attention apparently still fixed on the book on the bar top between his elbows. "When we were all in the business of selling just to the local people who have small farms and ranches hereabouts. And some few passengers who travel through on the stage. But with the coming of the railroad, also has come greed for many of us. And much money has been spent to make the town bigger in hope that—"

"Bruno, he is not a businessman, Mr. Edge." the older Linder cut in apologetically on the increasingly sour-toned voice of his son.

"I do not think bigger is always better and I consider the money expended on—"

"Damn glad all young American's don't think like you, kid," Meek growled. "or this country of ours'd still be just a bunch of states way back east and the rest of it carved up by a bunch of foreigners!"

The sheriff of Calendar finished his beer with an angry gesture—obviously irritated with himself for allowing the young Linder to provoke him. Perhaps in the latest of frequent heated discussions on the same subject. And Bruno looked up at last from his book, a smirking smile of triumph on his callow face, was about to press the needle harder into Meek when his father spoke first. In fast, harsh-sounding German accompanied by a grim frown. Which caused the boy to slam his book closed, straighten up, spin around and leave the saloon through a door between the end of the bar and the entertainment dais. After he had gone, his father became shame faced as he explained:

"I beg your pardon, gentlemen. I mean always never to speak German now I am American. I tell my son he is not a credit to the memory of his mother who shared my hopes and dreams and died in helping me to realize them. You see how this disgraces him?"

"Mrs. Linder was killed by Indians, Mr. Edge," Meek said pointedly, his self anger subdued now. "Ain't hardly any family here in Calendar that didn't lose one or more of its number on the wagon train from Independence that brought them all here. Them that have places out in the country to the south, too.

Edge had been slowly sipping his whiskey and beginning to relish the pleasant feeling of weariness it was helping to ease over his entire being. Said, having to stifle a yawn:

"Got the message out on the street awhile ago that this town holds a grudge against Indians, sheriff."

"I don't, personally. New here, along with the railroad and the expansion. Hired on to stop the kind of trouble you tried to start out on the street awhile ago."

Edge nodded. "Yeah, I have to admit I did start it."

"You like another beer, Mr. Meek?" Hans Linder asked eagerly, reaching for the empty glass the sheriff had replaced on the bar top.

"No!" the lawman said, snappishly, and waved a dismissing hand at the bartender in an angry gesture. Irritated by the interruption. "And that's not your usual style, I'd say?" he put to the half-breed. "Because I pride myself I can see beyond the outwards looks of people."

His dark eyes ran a tacitly eloquent survey over the seated length of the man at the table. And Edge remained just as silent for several seconds, like he had no comment to make to what Meek had said. Then he swallowed the few drops of rye that remained in the shot glass, and sighed as he replaced the stopper in the bottle.

"You're right, sheriff. It was real dumb of me

"You're right, sheriff. It was real dumb of me to start that play. Without knowing the feelings of the people here and how smart their lawman is."

"That isn't what I said, Mr. Edge. What interests me is why you provoked those two men so that one of them tried to get a gun—"

"Wasn't like it seemed, Mr. Meek," a man announced from the doorway as he pushed open the batwings. The disheveled undertaker who had been suspicious of Edge at first sight and now directed even more enmity toward the seated man as he halted just inside the threshold of the saloon.

"You want a drink, Mr. Downing?" Hans Linder asked eagerly.

"It wasn't, Cecil?" Meek asked.

The totally bald and almost toothless old man at the doorway shook his head. "No. Spenser claims he just took the rifles outta the box to show folks him and his partner had them to sell."

"Great sense of timin'," the sheriff growled.

"But that ain't what I come to tell you, Mr. Meek."

"It's not?"

Up at the railroad depot, a whistle shrilled. Blown by a man, not the locomotive. And maybe it was the same man who yelled into the silence the blast had heralded:

"Just advance news, folks! Figure to get the train rollin' in an hour! So she'll be ready to leave at eight o'clock! That's all, folks!"

Relief was expressed by many people out on

the street. And Marx began to talk loud and fast above the mass of voices, exhorting the crowd that there was still plenty of time to spend at the store on wheels.

"No, it ain't," Cecil Downing went on impatiently after the interruptions from outside. "I had my suspicions when I first seen this stranger roll into town, sheriff. That the buckboard he was ridin' and the mules that was haulin' it didn't belong to him."

"I, too, recognized that the animals which stop outside my saloon—" Linder begain, constantly nodding his head. But, unlike the undertaker, there was no rancor about the way he said it. Nor in the attitude of Meek as the lawman cut in:

"Seems certain of the local citizens don't appreciate as much as you do, Mr. Edge, that I still have at least the sense I was born with." He glanced over his shoulder at the bartender, who expressed chastened contrition. Then shifted his dark-eyed gaze to the down-at-heel man at the doorway, who was unrepentant but broodingly silent. Finally looked down at the half-breed as he continued: "Marc Maziol doesn't come to town as often as he used to. Can't afford to since the railroad took away most of his payin' customers. And doesn't have much of an inclination on account of not likin' people hereabouts for lobbying for the railroad."

"Exceptin' for me!" Downing put in vehemently. "Marc and me been checker playin' friends a lot of years and—"

"Except for Mr. Downin' here," Meek allowed. "But to get to the point. There's more than
one rundown old wreck of a buckboard still
bein' used in this part of the country. And more
than a single pair of mules. But there's just the
one pair of mules haulin' one old buckboard
that would make the first stop in Calendar—
come hell or high water—outside this saloon."

He looked questioningly at Edge as the smell
of smoke mixed with steam wafted in over and
under the batwings. Along with the sound of
the locomotive coming to life.

"Mules are a little like elephants, I guess.
They never forget."

"No doubt about it, Mr. Edge." The sheriff
nudged the half-breed's gear with the side of
his booted foot. Added: "Also no doubt that a
wagon isn't your usual way of travelin', seems
to me?"

"The Frenchman and I did a kind of trade,
sheriff," Edge supplied, no longer feeling
pleasantly weary. Sensing danger, but from beyond the confines of the cavernous saloon and
the three men he could clearly see.

"Kind of?" Meek posed.

"Left my horse there and took his wagon and
mules."

"Mr. Meek, I don't believe Marc would've
made a trade like that!" the undertaker complained, stroking the fires of hatred for Edge in
his weak looking eyes.

"He said a kind of trade," the lawman re-
minded, not shifting his gaze away from the
half-breed. And this implied demand for
further information was punctuated by a short,

sharp whistle, this time from the locomotive as the repairmen tested the build-up of steam.

"And it's a kind of truth he told, sir," a man announced from outside of the batwing doors, to draw the largely surprised attention of all four men in the saloon toward him. Three of the men recognizing the tall, thin, beak-nosed, red-haired, twenty year old kid who now eased open the slatted doors—with the barrel of a rifle that was aimed from the hip at the only member of the quartet who did not know him.

"You look like you just reached town, feller," the half-breed said, to fill the silence that Meek, Linder and Downing had expected the new-comer to fill.

"From the north, mister. By way of the Dora River at Frenchman's Crossin'."

He looked and sounded tough and sure of himself. Tired and dirt grimed from a long trip but not at all careless.

"Then you didn't hear me—"

"I heard enough, mister!" the youngster snarled and came through the batwings, to show that his finger was on the trigger and the hammer was cocked on the Winchester.

Edge went on as if there had been no inter-ruption: "—warn the people here that if a gun is aimed at me twice, the second time I do my damndest to kill the one that didn't listen to me."

"This is my deputy, Glenn Royale, Mr. Edge," Cy Meek said hurriedly as the young recent arrival looked ready to clash with the half-breed. 'What are you sayin', Glenn?"

The sheriff did not take his gaze away from

Edge after the brief glance at his deputy to see
the danger.

"There's a horse at Maziol's place all right,
Mr. Meek. Dead and half eaten by buzzards
and coyotes. Same as Maziol is. Least, I figure
it's Maziol. What's left of him is in a blanket on
my horse out front."

Hans Linder rasped: "*Mein Gott!*"

Cecil Downing snarled: "Sonofabitch!"

Cy Meek asked coldly: "Why?"

Edge answered: "He shot my horse instead
of me. And was fixing to rape—"

"Keep him covered, Glenn!" the lawman cut
in sharply, and came away from the bar to get
behind the seated half-breed. "You're under
arrest, Edge. For the time being. Until I find
out exactly what happened." He drew the
Frontier Colt from the holster as his suddenly
tougher looking deputy threw the stock of Winchester to his shoulder and aligned the sights
on the chest of his target, left of center. "Cecil,
go take care of the remains Glenn brought in.
Guess there's nobody more fittin' to make
formal identification of the decease."

There was a constant hissing of steam
through the escape valves of the locomotive
now and the air entering the Cottonwood
Saloon was heavier with its moist scent mixed
in with the more arid taint of woodsmoke. The
undertaker went out, careful not to get between the barrel of the rifle and Edge, and the
sheriff backed off from behind the prisoner,
pressing the confiscated revolver into the
waistband of his pants at the belly.

"Okay, on your feet, Edge," Meek said, sounding less tense now he had possession of the Colt. "We'll try to get this sorted out down at my office. Hans?"

"Yes, Mr. Meek?" Linder asked, nervous but also a little disappointed that he was not going to be a party to the rest of this incident.

"Keep an eye on Mr. Edge's gear. Glenn will be along to pick it up in a few minutes. Okay, Edge, head on out and don't let my deputy's youth fool you. He could kill you or cripple you over a lot greater distance than this. And I don't mean it would be a matter of your luck. Be his choice or my order."

"Something else I have to report, Mr. Meek," the deputy said, the muzzle of the rifle not wavering even fractionally as he turned and backed off so that the half-breed had a clear path to the doorway.

"What's that, Glenn?"

"The trees at Dora Spring are loaded with Indian dead."

"The trees?" Linder gasped, incredulous.

"It's the Arapaho way to bury the dead, Mr. Linder," the deputy answered. "They put the bodies up in the branches of trees."

"How disgusting!" a woman who had been eavesdropping outside exclaimed.

"Buzzards got to eat, the same as worms, lady," Edge said as he pushed between the batwings and saw a large group of local citizens and held-over train passengers on the center of the street. Between the saloon and the freight wagon where the two salesmen were in process of shutting up the store—the gathering perhaps just half the size as that which had been attracted to the sale.

"Murderer!" the matronly woman accused bitterly, frumpishly insulted by the half-breeds insensitivity to her sqeamishness. "I am sorry I must leave aboard the train! But I look forward to hearing that you have been hanged for your crime!"

"Everyone's entitled to their own opinions, lady," Edge countered as he turned out of the doorway to move along the street toward the sign that jutted from a building facade to announce that it was out front of the LAW OFFICE. "And mine is that no noose is good noose."

Chapter Nine

THE LAW office and jail were housed in a single story building with a flat roof on the west side of Calendar's only street, separated from the Railroad Hotel by a barber shop, bakery and the Presbyterian church. It was constructed at the front of timber and at the rear of red brick. The front section was a spartanly furnished but scrupulously clean office and at the rear there were three cells. A partition of floor to ceiling bars divided the two areas and there were also bars between the cells. There was a plate glass window, drape curtained to above eye level, beside the solid entrance door. And a single barred window, without glass, high in the rear wall—in the center cell. There were two desks, three chairs, a table, a rifle rack, a hatstand and a free standing closet in the office. In each cell there was just a narrow cot cemented into the floor with a straw mattress on top. These cots took up almost half the floor space of the cells.

The jail was one of the new additions to Calendar's facilities, built on at the rear of what had been a notions store that went bust. This detail of information was one of many concerning the development of the town that Sheriff Cy Meek gave to his only prisoner during a period when the lawman seemed reluctant to let silence reign in the place.

Official business was concluded for the night by then. Edge was stretched out comfortably on his back in the cell to the right, hat covering his face and sheepskin coat draped over him to serve as a blanket. He was fully dressed except for his boots and his gunbelt, which Meek had instructed his deputy to stow with the rest of the prisoner's gear—including his Colt and Winchester—in the closet. When this was done, the young lawman sat at his own desk on one side of the room and made a verbal report to the sheriff.

Meek interrupted Royale just once, when he held up a hand as he rose from his facing desk. And took from the top of the desk a shell ashtray that he pushed under the door into Edge's cell after the half-breed had rolled a cigarette and was about to strike a match on the brick wall to light it. Edge was sitting on the cot, his back into the angle of the corner, and he remained so while he smoked the cigarette, made careful use of the ashtray and listened to the red-haired young man.

It appeared that a local citizen out hunting had seen a sign that there was a large band of

Indians to the north west of Trio Bluff. And on instructions from Meek, Glenn Royale had left town two days earlier to check on the band's movements. He had picked up some tracks of Yellow Shirt's party and followed them on a wide swing, far to the west of the river's bend. It was an old trail, left when the Arapaho returned from a previous search for a suitable piece of land to settle. But it led back to the once well-established encampment that was now a burial place at the source of the river, called Dora Spring.

The deputy considered himself to be an expert tracker and knew there had been at least twice as many Arapaho camped at the Spring than were lodged in the trees nearby. But he failed to discover the direction in which the survivors had left after dealing with the dead. He did pick up another sign, though. That left by Edge's gelding dragging the travois—these tracks made not too long after a wagon and team had gone south from the encampment.

He had followed both set of signs to Frenchman's Crossing where he found the dead man and horse. The raft was missing and Royale had to swim his mount across the river. Where, for a mile and a half or so, the only reasonably fresh tracks on the trail were left by the wagon and team. But then a second rig had begun to leave a sign, after moving onto the trail from a patch of broken country to the east. Since both set of signs were leading from areas where trouble had struck toward the town where it

was his sworn duty to help keep the peace,
Deputy Royale had considered it best to make
for Calendar with all speed. Which is what he
did, spotting the dead Frenchman's buckboard
and mules outside the saloon and getting into a
position to hear what was being said just as the
half-breed seemed to be trying to pull the wool
over the sheriff's eyes in the matter of how
Marc Maziol died.

During the time that the deputy was making
his monotone report within the spartan confines of the office, there was a great deal of
quite noisy activity outside. Mainly concentra-
ted at the northern end of the street where passengers became eager for the train to leave and
the locomotive hissed and strained as if in
living sympathy with their feelings.

Now the gray-haired sheriff who had listened
with an attentive expression to his deputy,
asked Edge to give his account of events at
Dora Springs and Frenchman's Crossing. But
the prisoner and two lawmen had to wait to
talk and listen. For the train whistle shrilled,
the conductor yelled in competition with escaping steam that it was departure time and there
was the loudest burst of sound of all as the
reversing locomotive struggled from inertia to
push the line of cars out of the depot, over the
switchgear and across the trail toward the
north west. The barrage of noise resounding off
the face of Trio Bluff.

Only when he was able to speak at a normal
conversational level and be clearly heard did
the half-breed comply with Meek's request.

And gave a bald, concise account of his discovery of Nalin among the dead at the encampment, of their run-in with Marc Maziol, how the ferry raft was lost and what happened when Yellow Shirt and his band showed up at the night camp in the ravine.

Cy Meek listened to the even-voiced tale with the same level of attentiveness he had displayed when Glenn Royale was speaking. While the younger lawman who had previously directed only varying degrees of embittered resentment at the half-breed underwent a radical turnabout. And there was something akin to deferential admiration in his homely, unshaven and trail dirty face when Edge finished talking—as the train finally rolled beyond earshot.

Royale was obviously bursting with questions he wanted to ask. And perhaps was harboring some resentment toward Meek now, because of the way the senior man was handling the situation. But the older man beat the younger one to the vocal punch, as he rose from his desk and said:

"Okay, Glenn. Let's go. Whatever them Indians came to our piece of country for, what they're here for now is to kill whites. Fact they mean to take revenge for what happened to their people at the Spring is evidenced from the way they took such pains to cover their tracks."

"We gonna turn Mr. Edge loose and arrest them traders, sheriff?"

"Like hell we are, kid!" Meek answered bitterly and gestured for the deputy to lead the way to the door. "Let me tell you the facts of life about livin' in a town like Calendar."

They left the building, the sound of their footfalls and Meek's grumbling voice fading as the ceiling-hung kerosene lamp swayed through a gradually lessening arc after being set in motion by a draught of chill night wind when the door was briefly open. This stream of cold air entering the place emphasized the lack of a stove and it was then that Edge took off his topcoat and lay out on the coat, covering himself with the sheepskin and dropping his hat over his face to blot out the lamplight.

The only sounds that came into the law office from the vastness of the world beyond its walls were subdued by distance, perhaps identifiable if he had been inclined to attempt to recognize what they were. But he was not so inclined as he lay on the cot in this cell, waiting for the pleasing weariness he had experienced in the Cottonwood Saloon to permeate through his senses again.

A stream of disconnected thoughts and images came and went from his mind. Unbidden and some of them unwelcome. But on this occasion the half-breed made no attempt to put up a barrier against memories and neither did he feel moved to self anger in reflecting upon his actions since he first saw Nalin and how the responses she had triggered within him had influenced so much of what he had done.

She was, indeed, very beautiful. More beautiful, even, than the woman he had met and married and lost in such a tragically short space of time. More than enough time, for sure, to have planted the seed and for the initial growth of a new life to begin. But only to die before it was developed enough to be detected, when the life that gave it life was so cruelly ended.

At a thousand other times in a thousand different circumstances, Edge would have angrily tried to rid himself of such an uncharacteristic line of thought as this. But tonight it was as if his mind was as much a captive of strangers as was his physical being and he was totally resigned to acknowledging there was no chance of imminent escape. So best to ride the easiest route until he next had the opportunity to direct his own destiny.

Thus, for a few minutes, he was not as obstinate as Marc Maziol's mules. And was amenable to allowing that there were occasions when he experienced loneliness. Maybe sometimes was made a little crazy by the enormity of the space and the silence that surrounded him so often. But not so crazy as the Frenchman in his lust for the nubile body of Nalin . . .

The half-breed had never, for one moment, looked upon the seventeen year old girl in that way. Why, she had even chided him—good-naturedly as he recalled it—for his uncustomary display of shyness at the camp in the ravine. After she had accused him, in a temper, of being afraid to see and touch her injured breast.

Or was he remembering the interlude accurately? He vented a low grunt against the brim of his hat, dismissing the query. For he was not

voluntarily delving into the dark compart-
ments of times remembered with the express
purpose of reaching a conclusion about any
aspect of what had happened and why. He was
merely allowing his mind to wander at will
while he waited for sleep to come.

He had seen Nalin then as a beautiful face.
And beyond this as a young girl who was
wounded and in great distress. Who he had
helped. But why? Was it because he had known
that in a run-in with up to thirty revenge bent
Arapaho, he had a good chance of surviving
when they discovered he had helped one of
their kind? That was what she had accused and
it was the easy way out to look back and say he
was guilty of this.

But here in the peace and solitude of the Calendar jail, his free roaming mind had time and
opportunity to unearth the truth. And the
truth was that at the time he began to help the
young girl, he did so against her will. And he
was not so arrogant as to assume that he would
be able to alter her view in however long it took
for Yellow Shirt and his Arapaho braves to
locate them. So he had helped Nalin against her
will, which was not his way at all—went headlong against his basic philosophy that a man or
woman should be free to do exactly what he or
she wanted, provided they did not complain
when the time came to face up to the conse-
quences.

At the ferry, the Frenchman's intentions toward the young girl had done more to influence
Edge's reactions than the shooting of the

horse. Which again was not usual for this half-breed who claimed only to protect what was his —but by then it was too late. He had broken another fundamental rule of the way he led his life by entering into a relationship with another person.

Looking back now, he could see the bait in the trap. Placed there by the coincidences that were not quite perfect.

Nalin was not a half-breed by parentage; but because of circumstances she was not regarded by her own people as a full blood Arapaho squaw. She was the most beautiful young girl he had ever seen, but he never looked upon her as a woman. Not a coincidence, as such. But in retrospect, the way his mind was working tonight, he could recall no other woman—or girl— who had been there for the taking, and appealed to him, that he had not at least thought of taking . . . since Beth.

But Nalin was different from Beth. Nalin had been raised from an early age by a white couple. Like Josiah and Beth Hedges?

Damnit . . . he almost got angry then, as he was visited by the thought that it was only women who were supposed to get broody— women and hens and mares and . . . .

But then he smiled into the darkness of the inside of the crown of his hat, and perhaps there was a fire of warmth in his eyes as he felt his lips draw apart. For if a man could not laugh at himself, perhaps there was something wrong with him?

And maybe there was nothing wrong with a

man who, because of some mysterious response
felt a regard for a nubile young girl that was
entirely asexual, attempted to provoke a fight
in which he could kill the men who caused such
distress to the girl. Attempted to provoke such
a confrontation on a crowded street, to maybe
give the act some kind of respectability—
particularly as the representative of the law
was there to witness it?

Hell, it wasn't his way at all. Which is what
Cy Meek had said without being aware of the
emotions under the surface of the events. And
hell, if Beth had lived long enough to have a
child, it would not have been seventeen yet.
And, shit in hell, a father was supposed to want
a son.

Edge was too deeply engrossed in the stream
of increasingly nebulous thoughts and fragments of images that came and went from his
mind that he failed to hear the opening and
closing of the law office door, feel the fresh
draught of night air that was admitted or sense
the pressence of somebody else, until the
sheriff of Calendar asked harshly:

"You asleep, Edge?"

The half-breed took perhaps a full second to
come out of the emotional past and into the
present reality. Did not move from his comfortable position on the cot as he answered:

"No, sheriff. Figure you could say I've just
been brooding."

"Not like you or me to do that," the lawman
answered as he dropped into the chair behind
the desk.

"Even if fellers are on different sides of the law, they can be much the same."

Cy Meek vented a terse sound of disgust. Then growled. "You and me aren't on different sides, not really."

The half-breed felt a degree of expectancy in the silence, but made no offer to supply a comment. Or even raised his hat to look quizzically at the lawman.

"We all have to live, mister," Meek said at length, sounding just a little miffed. "And like I just told young Glenn Royale, those of us that had the opportunity to make our own beds got to consider ourselves real fortunate. And we also got to lie on them beds without whinin' when they get to feelin' a little lumpy. Don't you agree, mister?"

"I've been in a cell before, sheriff, and as beds go, this cot ain't so bad."

"Smart ass!" Meek snarled without too much rancor. "Why, if you sat on a thorn, I guess your brains could leak out."

"You're the real smart one, feller."

"I am?"

"You can walk out on me. But ain't no way I can escape hearing what you have to say."

There was a brief silence, then Meek clicked his tongue against the roof of his mouth and said morosely: "Like I agreed with young Royale, it's that Spenser and that Marx should be locked up in here. Because I don't doubt what the squaw said is true. They slaughtered more than a score of defenseless people. And you should be walkin' free. Because I know

what that no account ferryman was like—
wouldn't have been no shock to me if you'd
said he wanted to do away with you and the
squaw and rape your horse. But me and then
Glenn Royale, we hired on in Calendar as the
local people's lawmen. And like you got to
know, out here on the frontier, law's not all the
time applied accordin' to how it's written up in
the books.''

Once more there was a pause that was quite
obviously left by one man for the other to fill.
And Cy Meek was about to utter another
sound of irritation as a prelude to going on,
when Edge said from under his hat:

''Been my experience that it's not just out on
the frontier that people get the law they can
best afford.''

''Up your ass, mister!''

''Careful you don't damage my brains.''

Meek caught his breath, clicked his tongue
and sighed. Then continued, in a carefully controlled voice:

''Wherever you do your thinkin' from, Edge,
I figure you're bright enough to have got my
message. Calendar folks are anti-Indian and because of that they figure the men that killed all
the Arapaho are heroes. Whatever Calendar
folks thought about that crazy Frenchman who
ran the ferry, they have you marked down as
an Indian lover and so you have to stay on ice
to stand trial when the circuit judge next visits
town.''

There was a much longer silence between the
two men now. A time of utter peace, with not

even a single cicada chirping out in the chill of the night. Broken when Edge said:

"Sheriff?"

"Yeah?"

"Circuit judge be by before the Indians hit this town?"

"Guess not. But Glenn Royale figured about twenty-five to thirty braves."

"He's about right."

"We have men posted to watch for an attack from any side of town. And any man who isn't sleepin' with a gun at his bedside tonight knows where can lay hands to one pretty damn soon. There are more than fifty men between eighteen and sixty-five in town and on the farmsteads to the south."

"So I can sleep easy in my bed."

"We got blankets if you want."

"No thanks, sheriff."

"Hope to get a stove in here sometime. Place used to be a notions store until it was converted and they added on the cells. Never did replace the stove after they knocked down the rear wall that used to be and . . ."

Cy Meek continued to talk, holding a one way conversation with an unresponsive listener who might well have been quietly sleeping for all the interest he showed in the potted history of Calendar that was related to him. Then, eventually, the lawman ran out of fresh information on his subject or the inclination to deliver an unappreciated monologue on anything. And he rose from the desk, went to the hatstand, donned a frockcoat cape-fashion over his shoulders and sat down again. Pressed his cupped hands to his mouth and breathed warm, expelled breath into the palms. Then muttered:

"Damnit, I should've insisted they put a stove in this place!"

And Edge growled from under his hat: "Yeah, sheriff. Thing's around here ain't too hot, are they?"

Chapter Ten

EDGE WAS in a dreamless sleep in the small hours of the cold morning and he came awake easily. Was not jolted into awareness by the distant sound that his sixth sense for danger warned him might well portend fresh violence.

But the first sound he heard while consciously listening was the whistling end of another man's snore. Instantly knew where he was and why he was there. Knew also, before he folded up on the cot, swung his feet to the floor and put his hat on the top of his head, that it was Sheriff Cy Meek doing the snoring or else the two lawmen of Calendar, New Mexico snored in exactly the same way. They didn't. It was the sparsely framed, gray-haired, burnished-faced older of the two peace officers who was sleeping in his chair, folded forward so that his head rested on his arms folded on the top of his desk. Clear to see because Meek had only turned the kerosene lamp down and not out when he aban-

doned attempts to start a rap session with a
man who had apparently gone to sleep—and
settled down to sleep himself. Now, in the
diminished level of lamplight the lawman who
was more in sympathy with his prisoner than
the citizens of Calendar who paid him, continued to sleep peacefully in his uncomfortable
posture. Snoring in a subdued way as Edge put
on his sheepskin coat and then leaned into the
angle of the side and rear wall of the cell, while
he listened to the far off sound that had to
travel many miles through the still dark night
to reach him.

Correctly identified now—as it got closer and
louder sounding not in the least like a distant
roll of thunder in a storm that might perhaps
move in any direction. Thunder rolls came and
went. This rumbling sound, now that the half-
breed was wide awake, was continuous.

Edge struck a match on the cell wall and lit
his cigarette. Dropped the dead match in the
shell ashtray Meek had provided and rasped
the back of a hand over the thick growth of
bristles on his jaw. The noise of this masked
the sound far out in the night—as did the snoring of the lawman every few seconds or so. But
not for long. Because the source of the distur-
bance to the night time peace to the north west
of Calendar was a train heading for town and
coming in at high speed.

Meek coughed himself awake after he unwit-
tingly sucked in some of the smoke from the
half-breed's cigarette. So came awake noisily
and irritably, stiff from his awkward posture

and disconcerted by not knowing where he was for a few seconds.

Voices were raised out along the street, calling questions and giving replies. In tones of excitement, nervousness and perplexity. The sheriff was still unhappy at his rude awakening as he fisted the grit of sleep from his dark eyes and glowered at the composed and impassive half-breed to demand:

"What the hell's happenin', Edge?"

"There's a train coming in from the north west, feller. And from the way its stirred the people up around here I'd guess it's not a scheduled arrival."

While the half-breed was giving his even-voiced reply, Meek listened also to the noises from near and far outside. And dug a watch from a pocket under his topcoat—had to tilt the face to the meager light from the lamp to read the time.

"It's five in the mornin', damnit!" he growled as he thrust the watch back under his coat and knocked his chair over backwards in his haste to rise from the desk. "No train due at Calendar until midday!"

"Going to be real early," Edge said. "Even if the engineer does slow her down some."

"Trouble, it's gotta be," Meek rasped as he went around his desk, to get a rifle from the rack before he headed for the door.

Which was pushed open before he could reach it. And the overweight Hans Linder blocked the way out, breathless from running, a worried frown on his pale face as he held a

Winchester rifle across his chest and belly in a two-handed, knuckle-whitening grip.

"Just come down from the station, Mr. Meek!" he reported, rushing out the words between gasps for breath. "Your young assistant said I should watch for Indians from there. But it is not Indians I see coming. It is a train."

"Yeah, Hans, I hear it," Meek said, a little impatiently as he made to leave the office. But the way remained blocked by the stout frame of the German bartender.

"The station manager, Mr. . . . ."

"Flohr, Hans."

"*Ja*, that is right. Mr. Flohr is awakened by the noise of the train coming and comes out of his house to the station in his night shirt. And he says for me to come and bring you, Mr. Meek. For the train, it is not only unscheduled. It is traveling too fast and unless the engineer quickly—"

"Outta my way, mister!" the lawman snarled as his patience with the breathless but still garrulous man finally ran out. And he shouldered his way between Linder and the doorframe to join the rapidly swelling crowd of people hurrying along the street—everyone heading for the north end of it. The shouted questions, counter questions and answers and the thud of footfalls still audible against the increasing volume of sound from the hurtling train.

"What do you think, feller?" Edge asked as Linder made to turn and join his fellow citizens after several moments of uneasily not knowing what to do.

"Mr. Edge?" he countered, puzzled.

"Could you see the train?"

"Just the smoke."

"A runaway, you figure?"

The bulky shoulders were shrugged while the puzzled frown remained on the fleshy face of the bartender. "Mr. Flohr fears this. When he has told me to come to the law office and bring the sheriff, he takes a telescope up onto the roof of the depot building, Mr. Edge. The better to see the train that is coming so fast to town."

Linder was having to speak louder to make himself heard above the relentlessly rising volume of sound from the approaching locomotive—that masked the noise of everything else that was taking place outside the law office. Speeding wheels clattered along track, steam rushed from outlet valves, slipstream roared along the sides and over the top of the locomotive and in imagination it could seem possible to hear the crackle of the cordwood that was blazing in the firebox and even the straining of metal plates against their rivets as they were subjected to pressures they were not designed to withstand.

"Maybe while he's up there, Flohr will figure out a way to—"

"I can't hear what you're saying, Mr. Edge!" the bartender roared, but made no move to get closer to the cell in which the half-breed was imprisoned—instead felt the compelling need to leave the law office and see what inevitably was going to happen now that there was no sound of screeching brakes.

And he submitted to this overwhelming urge

to satisfy his eager curiosity just as Edge said
around the bobbing cigarette:

"Was remarking that the railroadman might
get ideas above his station, feller."

It was a bad joke made at a bad time, but
was heard by nobody. Just as there was no one
in a position to see Edge's mirthless grin of
exposed teeth and glittering eyes as he spoke
the unheard words into the tumultuous barrage of sound that filled the Calendar night. To
reach a crescendo of evil pandemonium over a
period of stretched seconds, which subsided a
great deal faster than it erupted and was followed by an enormous surrounding peace punc-
tured at irregular intervals by sounds in isola-
tion.

There was just the locomotive that had been
repaired at the Calendar depot a few dark
hours earlier. Minus the string of cars as it
thundered back to town at a raging speed that
placed it in danger of derailment over every
yard of track as rails and ties and spikes and
even rock bed beneath the permanent way
vibrated. Threatened to bend, shift, fly free or
collapse under the hurtling weight of what
everybody in town now knew to be a runaway.
This fact made patently evident as the engine
came around the final curve of the track, left
the moon-shadowed base of the south west
facing cliff of Trio Bluff and started down the
final straightaway to town. Fifty, sixty,
seventy or maybe even a hundred miles an
hour. It was impossible for anybody who saw
the engine, smoke and steam streaming out

behind, to guess at the speed it was making as it closed from the arrowhead shaped point of the bluff with the buffer of sand in a box at the end of the line.

Many watched, spellbound and seemingly rooted to the spot where they were at the moment they realized the engine was not going to halt. While others whirled from hurrying toward the depot to break into faster runs away from it. And a handful, seeing the danger without being fascinated by it, pulled at or shouted at those who were reluctant to move or were mesmerized.

The speed of the engine that suddenly looked much bigger than it was, could now be felt as well as seen and heard—the vibrations it created transmitted from track to street. And the ground and some of the buildings which stood on it trembled as if from the initial shock wave of an earthquake.

Then the cowcatcher hit the buffer and both —never constructed to withstand a fraction of such an impact—were destroyed in a part of a second. Pieces of splintered timber and shards of shattered metal hurled high into and through the air in a spray of exploded sand.

And the pace of the runaway at last was reduced. But only marginally at first, after the wheels had left the rails and were captured by a far harsher element of drag as the rims bit into the hard-packed dirt of the street.

Two of Calendar's citizens were dead by then, a man hit in the heart by a piece of metal that penetrated his flesh with the velocity but

not the neatness of a bullet, and a woman who
took a blow on the head with a length of wood
hard enough to shatter her skull. Their screams
of fear were immediately curtailed and they
had no time to vent agony. More than a score of
other people continued to utter their vocal responses to the horror of the runaway as,
without exception now, they all raced to clear
the path of the engine. Which maintained a
high rate of speed as much by thrusting momentum as by the power of steam under pres-
sure as its entire length and all eight wheels
left the track. For twenty yards or so, the
engine continued to run straight and if there
had been time for them to consider it, the
people who had angled to either side might
have felt relief that they were safe.

But then the two pairs of leading wheels suddenly wrenched away from the straight. This
as the engine roared across the front of the
restaurant, trailing dust as well as smoke and
steam now. And the engine veered to the left,
visibly slowed by the switch from track to dirt
—seemed on the point of smashing through the
false front of the Cottonwood Saloon, perhaps
to come to rest in the wreckage of what had
once been the Linders' place or maybe to run
itself to a standstill in the open country out
back. But the wheels had turned too sharply, to
demand that the engine take a curve that was
impossible to achieve.

The damaged front of the engine clipped the
far front corner of the saloon, crushing the too-
terrified-to-move Otis Snyder who had been

intent on plunging into the alley beside the place before the engine slowed to the side. The two wheels on the right side buckled under the weight of the reluctant-to-turn length of engine and the entire thing tilted in the direction of the buckled wheels—and the diagonally opposite rear one came clear of the ground. When, just for a moment, the drive wheels maintained traction before the forward thrust was transferred to the side and the engine's center of gravity changed. And it rolled. Onto its side, over on its back, on its other side and back up onto its wheels again. But only to go through the same destructive turn once more after the drive wheels, fed less power, failed to move the engine forward against the skewed around and buckled steering wheels.

This power was lessened because the fire box door had sprung open and flaming cordwood spilled out. Scalding water gushed from the boiler tank, too. And steam hissed from safety valves. Much that was vital to the running of the locomotive incapable of operating while it was rolled through a three hundred and sixty degree turn. Then another. And another. The engine going diagonally across the street from the saloon toward the church. Burning and scalding a woman and two men caught out in the open and unable to shelter from the downpour of flames and water. And setting fire to the roof of the bakery between the barber shop and the church.

The cacophony of sound was as loud as ever and was comprised of different combinations of

noise now—of destruction rather than of speed
as the stricken locomotive came finally to rest.
Like some once-proud beast taken out of its element to be brutally slaughtered after putting
up a valiant fight. It lay on its side, cabin outside the arched porchway of the church and
crumpled smokestack pointed at the law office
next door. The engine crackled and hissed and
snorted and spat, for several moments almost
totally hidden in the outpourings of its own
vapors.

Then it exploded.

Just as the cries of the injured, the screams
of the terrified and the anger of those demanding an end to the bedlam started to be heard
through the din, every other sound in the world
was blotted from hearing or shocked into non-
existence by the massive roar of the engine
blowing itself apart. Upwards and outwards
the smoke and the flame billowed and leapt.
Touching much but harming nobody. Scorch-
ing some building fronts was all. But an
instant later, ragged pieces of metal plating
and sheered off bolts, shards of glass and complete components were hurled through the suddenly hot, no longer clear night air. Amid foun-
tain sprays of sparks. None of this going so far
and wide as the fire and smoke, but spreading
more damage.

The unambitious Bruno Linder was decapi-
tated by a toothed wheel that sliced through
his flesh as he knelt beside a woman who had
fainted. His head rolled to a halt at the front of
the saloon before his blood gushing torso top-

pled to the ground. As the woman recovered only to be plunged back into unconsciousness by this new shock.

Flohr, still clutching his telescope, was almost cut in half by one of the stricken locomotive's drive wheels as he raced, trance-like, toward the explosion. And the wheel that had killed the railroadman continued to roll, slick with his blood, until it smashed through the doorway of the hotel.

Three other Calendar citizens were injured by flying debris and a number of buildings had windows blown out by blast. And the church was on fire, the blaze started by a vicious shower of sparks. While a few feet away, there was a jagged hole where the window and frame of the law office had been—caused by the torn free smokestack as it smashed from engine to building like a massive artillery shell.

The harsher and louder sounds of the train wreck and its havoc were diminished and voices, many of them calm, could be heard again through the crackle of flames consuming the church timbers and the clicking noises of hot metal cooling—plus the less strident screams and not so demanding moans of the injured and afraid. This as smoke from the fire at the church rolled and billowed across the street more thickly than had that from the locomotive a little earlier.

People ran from the places where they had taken shelter from the out-of-control engine to give help to the wounded and cover the dead. To begin to fight the fire and to find out if their

near and dear ones not immediately seen were
all right.

All this taking place out in the open while,
inside the law offices, Edge struck a match on
the rear wall of his cell and relit the part-smok-
ed cigarette angled from a side of his mouth.
Then rose from the cot rock steady on his feet
as his heavily bristled face continued to be
totally impassive. The ice cold glint in his
narrowed eyes presenting the truth about the
state of his feelings as he reached forward with
an unshaking hand to push open the door of the
cell. Stepped through and went to the closet in
which he had seen Glenn Royale stow his gear.
He took out just his Colt which he slid into the
holster and his Winchester which he canted to
his left shoulder.

He had to stoop to do this for the free standing closet had been toppled over and broken
open. Just as Cy Meek's desk and the chair in
front of and behind it had been knocked off
their legs. But they had been crushed and
splintered by the hurtling smokestack after it
smashed in through the window and before it
came to rest against the bars of the center cell.
Had hit the bars with enough force to snap
some and bend others. The damage severe at
the point of impact and less so to either side.
But the bending effect nonetheless transmitted across the entire width of the partition by
horizontal bars. The distortion pronounced
enough for the tongue of the lock to be drawn
out of the bracket so that the half-breed had

been able to swing open the door without need of a key.

It was not a way he would have chosen to set himself free for the smokestack might have crashed into and through the bars of his cell. And any one of the fragments of window glass that now crunched beneath his booted feet might have severed a vital artery. But in a situation such as this, it was never his way to concern himself with what might have been. There had been too many occasions when he could have been blown to bits, crushed to death or seen his life's blood pouring out of him. And if to escape death yet again was his lot, then he accepted it without pause for thought upon it. And took advantage of the bonus of freedom and the opportunity this provided for him to have some control over the outcome of his next run-in with violence.

Which he guessed would not be long in coming. But did not arrive with Glenn Royale as the young deputy appeared at the hole in the wall where the law office window had once been. To peer into the darkness of the no longer lamplit interior from an area spread with flickering light from the burning church.

"Mr. Edge?" he called tentatively.

"Guess your boss is going to be real mad about the mess in here, feller."

"Why, how—" Royale started, his voice shrill with startlement.

"The runaway train came around the hill instead of over it. But she sure as hell blew."

"Kid, we got the church and the bakery on fire!" Cy Meek bellowed from up the street. "Lend a hand here, why don't you!"

"But, sheriff—"

"He's either dead or he'll keep!" Meek cut in on the deputy.

"If he won't listen, he can't be told," Edge said. His voice calm, but the Winchester adding a tacit threat as he swung it down from his shoulder and across the front of his body, to take a two-handed grip on it. Not yet aimed at the unhandsome, no longer capable looking young lawman who remained undecided for a few moments more.

Then Royale rasped: "If I can't see nothin', I can't tell him nothin'."

"Much obliged," the half-breed said as the deputy turned and ran toward the fires and he moved forward, to swing a leg up and over what remained of the wall below what had once been the draped window. Brought his trailing leg over the same obstacle and then froze to the sound of a rifle shot and a shout.

A great many other people out on Calendar's only street were fleetingly held in unmoving attitudes by the twin sounds. Then heads were wrenched from side to side as the direction from which the unexpected shot and the accompanying shout had come was sought. Before almost everyone stared toward the northern end of the street. From where a man was running, his rifle held in a one-handed grip at arms length in the air with smoke still wisping from its muzzle. And in the silence, broken only by the crackle of flames, which had gradually settled over the town after the crack of the rifle shot, the running man's voice sounded with shocking clarity when he yelled:

"Injuns! The Injuns! The Injuns are comin'!"

Like everyone else in Calendar, Edge heard the frightened announcement. But he did not see the man who made it. And neither did the overweight Jason Spenser and the stockily built Eddie Marx. Who were watched in silence for long seconds by the half-breed as they hurried to harness the team to their wagon out back of the livery stable, some three hundred feet away from the rear of the law office and jail.

Edge covered two hundred and fifty of these feet in the moon shadow of the buildings, any sound he made masked by the chorus of raised voices out on the street. Then he paused, in moon shadow still and with questions and answers continuing to fill the night that was cold again out here beyond the reach of the flames. Waited until the two fast working salesmen had completed their chore and the florid-faced Marx moved around the front of the team to join the sad-eyed Spenser on this side of the garishly painted wagon.

When he went forward again, taking long strides, with the Winchester thrust out in front of him. Marx was already half up on to the footboard of the wagon and Spenser was rasping at him to hurry—when they both sensed danger. And the man on the ground started to swing

around, reaching for a revolver that was
pushed into the waistband of his suit pants at
his belly. But the barrel of the half-breed's rifle
clubbed him viciously across the side of the
head and sent him into a reverse turn as he
corkscrewed to the ground and vented a hissing sound of escaping breath.

This as Eddie Marx rasped an obscenity and
reached with both hands for a rifle under the
seat of the wagon. When Edge said:

"You heard the man, feller," and moved his
Winchester in a bayoneting action this time—
to smash the muzzle hard into the crotch of the
hapless Marx. Who gasped and fell backwards
off his insecure perch, empty hands clawing
toward the source of his agony. And Edge
swung away to the side as he used the rifle as a
club again, but made contact with the stock
against the side of this man's head while he
was falling. So that Marx was unfeelingly unconscious as he slammed hard down beside his
partner. "The Indians are coming and I'm
starting to breath a little heavy," the half-
breed added in a growling tone. "But without
you there won't be any climax."

Chapter Eleven

MARX AND Spenser did not have rope as a
stock in trade, but there was plenty of it in the
livery and Edge used his razor to cut as much
as he needed from somebody's lariat. Then he
cut this into three lengths and used two of
these to lash the wrists of the unconscious men
—behind their backs. The third and longest
piece he used to link the prisoners together, by
the wrists but with enough slack so that when
they recovered they would be able to stand and
to walk side by side.

All this took perhaps three minutes to
achieve and while he was tying up the men the
half-breed shot frequent glances about him—
wary of being seen and even attacked by the
local citizens rather than being concerned,
right now, about the Arapaho. But only he
moved stealthily out back of the buildings on
the west side of Calender's one street. While
the townspeople, calming and quieting down

after an initial response that came close to
panic, gravitated to the north end of the street.
Beyond the wrecked locomotive and the blazing buildings—the fires that were consuming
them no longer being fought with pails of
water. So that the unchecked flames raged and
roared, radiating a bright and constantly moving light that reached to and fell across the
crowd of perhaps a hundred people gathered on
the end of the street between the railroad depot
and the row of railroad company houses.

People who, for some time may have been inclined to accuse the man who fired off his rifle
and yelled the warning of seeing nothing more
substantial than shadows out at Trio Bluff.
But nobody did, for it had been realized that
the locomotive which caused such terror, death
and destruction had hurtled off the end of the
track and into Calendar without a driver on
the footplate. So had not been accidentally
wrecked by somebody in a desperate attempt
to warn the townspeople of an Arapaho attack.

Instead, the engine had been started toward
town with a full head of steam and a roaring
firebox with the deliberate intention of causing
as much damage as possible. This as the initial
blow of an Indian attack. But one that was not
going to be started immediately, it soon became apparent.

But there was definitely activity out there
under cover of the moon shadow from the
south west facing side of the bluff. Just beyond
the point where the railroad track curved and
was lost to sight in the same area of darkness.

"I seen an Injun for sure!" the man who gave the warning blurted defensively to end a lengthy vocal silence during which the night had been disturbed only by the sounds of the buildings burning down.

"Ain't nobody doubtin' you, Fred," a woman assured.

"What you figure they got in mind to do, Mr. Meek?" Glenn Royale asked.

"Only one thing's sure about that, kid," the sheriff growled. "That we folks won't like what it is."

"Ain't that the truth."

"How many you figure?"

"Glenn and Mr. Edge say about thirty."

"Well, we outnumber them, even if we don't include the women."

"Could be them redskins out there have somethin' up their sleeves that don't take account of any head-on fight, George."

"Somethin' like the folks that was in the cars that were strung to the engine when it left here last night, Mr. Meek?"

"Had a crew aboard the train, too," a railroadman pointed out.

There was a short lull in the talk as the townspeople considered the implications of fighting Indians who held hostages. And the men with rifles tightened their grips on them while those with holstered revolvers draped hands over the butts. Some recalling old fights with the Indians and some thinking only of the current trouble which had started so violently.

"Could be everyone was slaughtered when

the savages stopped the train, Mr. Meek."

"Wouldn't have gone down without puttin'
up a fight, neither!" a railroadman said with
determination. "So could be there ain't so
many Injuns out there as the deputy and the
stranger reckon on."

This suggestion triggered a whole buzz of
talk that acted to relieve some of the tension
that had built during the lull. But there were
few in the throng who allowed their attention
to be drawn away from the moon shadow under
the bluff—willing to discuss what might
happen, but not ready to risk missing the first
sign of the Arapaho's next move.

Sheriff Cy Meek was one of those who did
shift his attention away from Trio Bluff, when
Deputy Glenn Royale said in a rasping whisper
no one else could hear:

"Reckon you should know the prisoner's out,
sheriff."

The older lawman looked grimly into the concerned face of the youngster for as long as it
took him to demand: "How?" Then he peered
out along the trail and railroad track again.

"Couldn't see clear, sir. But I guess there's a
chance that whatever tore the hole in the front
of the office busted down the bars."

Meek nodded shortly and muttered: "Saves
me goin' back to the office and lettin' him out,
kid. He's the kind of guy who can handle himself in a fight and that's the kind we're goin' to
be needin'."

"He ain't here, Mr. Meek. I been lookin' for
him, but I ain't seen a sign of him since you
told me to help fight the fire."

The sheriff's burnished face was fleetingly visited by a look of anger before it became merely grim again and he growled: "So maybe he don't want to mess in other folks' troubles."

"Somethin' else, sheriff."

"Yeah, kid?"

"While I been lookin' for Edge, I also been noticin' them two traders ain't around either."

"I noticed that, too."

"And since there ain't no doubt but they're the reason for what's happenin', I reckon they should lend a hand here."

"Sheriff!"

"I see him, Fred," Cy Meek said into the silence that had gripped the crowd in the wake of the anxiously spoken word as everyone saw what had caused the exclamation.

The appearance of a lone figure at the southernmost point of Trio Bluff—moving out along the railroad track in an awkward gait on the ties. Between rails that no longer glinted so sharply in the lessening light of the moon as the first grayness of the false dawn made inroads against the dark of night. Then the shadowless, soft light of the new day could be seen to perceptibely increase as the figure moved to more than fifty feet beyond the point of the bluff. There to come to a halt, hands hanging low at his sides and empty.

The same light of dawn acted to dim the flames of the fires that had now burned low within the ruined church and bakery. But nobody in the town that smelled so strongly of burning paid any attention to the dying fires. Nor to the increasing level of light spreading across the sky from the east. Nor even, after he had come to a halt, to Chief Yellow Shirt.

Instead, every gaze was fixed upon the scene in back of the lone Arapaho—in which two files of braves were stooped and straining as they emerged into the open. One column to either side of the track, hauling on lengths of rope that were tied to the coupling of a railroad day car. Also tied to the car were six corpses. Three strung up along each side of the car by ropes noosed around their necks and running over the roof. But the four men and two women had not died by hanging, for the blood of bullet or blade wounds stained their clothing. There was a lot of dried blood, too, on their heads and faces from where they were scalped.

Gasps and cries, some obscenities and a few pleas to God, the thud of a fainted woman hitting the ground and the clicking of several gun hammers being cocked were the low volume sounds which rose from the tight-knit crowd of watching men and women as they saw the gruesome tableau placed before them. Then a new and more tense silence gripped the people of Calendar as the car was rolled to a halt by the sixteen braves on the ropes, perhaps ten feet in back of where the patient and resolute figure of Yellow Shirt stood.

It was light enough now for the waiting throng to see what was happening behind the car, at the base of the bluff. Where the remainder of the band of Arapaho sat their ponies, some of them holding the reins of the mounts of the braves who had hauled the car into view—and who now abandoned the ropes and returned to join the mounted men. And one woman.

Reins were handed from brave to brave and then every Arapaho except for Yellow Shirt was astride a pony. And then every mounted Arapaho except for Nalin heeled his pony forward. Some to the left and some to the right of the railroad car with its gristly appendages. An equal number to either side who reined in their ponies when they were level with their chief. Thirty Arapaho in all, including Yellow Shirt and Nalin. The whole large group suddenly as silent and unmoving as the larger number of Calendar citizens after the line of ponies was halted.

The whites with hands on guns or close to them. The Indians unthreatening for the moment in the way their rifles were slung across their backs and their hands remained almost pointedly far away from their weapons belts.

The silence was absolute to the many human ears for the stretched seconds while the light of the rising sun and then the leading arc of the sun itself made an impression on the landscape that would have been virtually featureless had it not been for Trio Bluff, Calendar and the twin rails—once more glinting brightly—that connected them.

"Hell, what are they waitin' for?" Cecil Downing snarled and did not quite manage to mask his fear.

"For somebody here to make the first move, way I see it," Edge answered, not needing to raise his voice much higher than normal to be heard by everybody grouped between the hotel and the restaurant. So solid was the silence under the bright, cold light of the new sun which was then broken again by the shuffling of feet and the venting of fresh sounds of shock as the Calendar citizens turned to peer at the half-breed—and open up a corridor for him to pass through. He and his two charges.

Edge, in back of the tied up and tied together Eddie Marx and Jason Spenser, was several yards away from the crowd—just passing the overturned locomotive—when he made his response to the disreputable looking undertaker. Having waited patiently for his captives to recover consciousness out back of the livery stable. Then forced them to be quiet—if not patient—by aiming the Colt at Marx and the Winchester at Spenser until Yellow Shirt called the first play. Then, again with the tacit threats of the two guns to urge quiet compliance with his demands, the half-breed had directed the helpless men down the alley between the livery and a dry goods store and to make a left turn on to the street. The three of them undetected by anybody until he spoke the even-toned comment that drew such startled attention to the prisoners and himself.

"So nobody ran out?" Cy Meek said, a little huskily, as he swung around, to put his back to the distant band of Arapaho and face the captives and captor at the end of the pathway between the two sides of the crowd.

"There was a rumor?" Edge asked, aware of

people closing the gap behind him, but making no attempt to emphasize the already patently obvious fact that the revolver in his right hand was just a foot or so away from the spine of Spenser while the muzzle of the rifle sometimes brushed against the back of the other trader's suit jacket.

"Me and Jase figured to draw off the Indians, sheriff!" Marx blurted as he and his partner were forced to come to a halt in front of Meek, who was now joined by Royale—neither lawman moving his rifle away from its aim at the cloudless, sun-bright sky. "It's us they want and no fight of Calendar people. This drifter jumped us and laid his rifle over our heads before he would explain why he was hitching up our team."

"Can see where he assaulted you guys, all right," the sheriff murmured, wincing as he briefly looked at the contusions on the sides of their heads. "What do you have to say to that, Mr. Edge?"

"Mr. Edge, shit!" Downing snarled. "He's an escaped prisoner and an Injun lover to boot!"

"Cecil, there's no excuse for the use of such language and—"

"Guilty of laying my rifle across their heads, sheriff," the half-breed cut in on the preacher's castigation of Downing. "And if anybody makes a move to change the way I've got these fellers—"

"I was meanin', what you got to say about their story they was figurin' to lead the Indians away from town?" Meek interrupted.

"More likely to believe that the sun won't
like the look of things around here and will
slide back the way it came."

There was a hubbub of rasping talk, all of it
in tones of enmity. But nothing could be heard
clearly and it was impossible to tell if the dis-
like was directed at Edge or the two traders.
And since all three were watching only the
sheriff, there was no opportunity for a visual
check. Then the uneasy exchanges were curtailed when Meek nodded and said:

"Guess you know I go along with you in
figurin' these guys were wrong to shoot up the
Indian camp?"

"Me, too!" Glenn Royale added quickly.

And there was another burst of dissatisfied
talk—indicating that the vast majority of
Calendar citizens were on the side of the two
murdering traders.

"Shut up, kid, and shut up the rest of you!"
Meek snapped, not shifting the fixed gaze of
the dark eyes away from the glittering slits of
the half-breed's blue ones. "But that don't
mean I'm goin' to stand back and see you hand
these guys over to Arapaho mercy, mister.
Tied up the way they are. Or any way. Unless
they agree to be exchanged for the train passengers that ain't hangin' on the outside of the
car."

Now he did glance momentarily to the left
and right inviting a response from the prisoners. His unchanged expression of grim determination suggesting he already knew what the
reply would be.

"Like hell we agree!" Spenser muttered.

"On the run, aboard our wagon, we had a chance, Mr. Meek!" Marx added hurriedly. "But we aren't about to commit suicide."

"Right," Edge said. "Unless the sheriff and his deputy get out of the way, you are about to get murdered. Same thing if anyone without a badge tries to stop me doing what I have in mind."

"What you got in mind, mister?" Spenser demanded to know tremulously as he saw the look of resignation under the grimness of Meek's sun-ravaged face.

"Hey, sheriff!" the ever-observant Fred called anxiously. "Things are movin'."

Edge looked between the heads of his two prisoners and Meek and Royale, out along the track to where the line of Arapaho braves continued to sit stoically astride their ponies at either side of their chief.

Hans Linder, red-eyed and gaunt-looking as he grieved for his dead son, said from close to the half-breed. "He has his fingers on the triggers of the guns, Mr. Meek. I do not think we can—"

"Yeah, Hans," the lawman cut in. "And a mind made up to do what he has to do." He raked his dark-eyed gaze over the grim faces of the tense townspeople and warned: "Anyone tries anythin', they'll kill Edge, sure enough. But that won't do anythin' to save the lives of these other two strangers."

Meek looked hard into the impassive face of the half-breed for a stretched second, like he was tacitly pleading for an assurance that he was doing the right thing. But he learned nothing before he turned and stepped out of the way, gesturing with a jerk of his head that Royale should do the same. And the young deputy did so, and two of them to peer out at the slightly different scene at the point of the bluff.

The movement Fred had spotted was of Nalin riding her pony out from under the early morning shade of the cliff, swinging wide to go around the line of mounted braves to Yellow Shirt's right. And now she completed the slow ride—reached the center of the line at the front and got smoothly down from the back of the pony. Pressed the rope reins into the out-stretched hand of the chief. Then turned and, choosing not to walk on the awkwardly spaced ties or the broken rock of the rail bed, started toward town at the side of the track.

"Let's go meet the lady, fellers," Edge instructed, and nudged the rifle muzzle against the back of Eddie Marx.

"Sheriff?" the city-suited trader pleaded huskily.

"That the squaw you helped, Mr. Edge?" Meek asked.

"Yeah."

"I'd rather you blast us here and now than be handed over to those savages," Jason Spenser said tautly.

"No sweat to kill you," Edge replied evenly.

"No!" Marx rasped, head snapping around

to direct a pleading look up at his taller partner.

"No," Meek echoed, a good deal calmer, peering in turn at Spenser, Edge and Marx. Then hardened his tone and expression as he promised: "Nobody's goin' to get handed over to the Indians. This isn't just somethin' I use to scare folks with." He moved his rifle up from where he carried it across the base of his belly and then lowered it again. "It's a tool of my trade that I know how to use. And if the worst happens, I'll use it on you two. First, if you get my drift?"

He continued to look at the captives and captor in turn as he spoke—and finished with a fixed look of determination at Edge.

"She's stopped, sheriff," Fred reported.

"You mean this is some kind of trick you're pulling on the Indians, mister?" Eddie Marx asked, hope in his voice and his florid face.

The half-breed's nod to the sheriff was barely perceptible, and did not reveal if he was acknowledging his understanding of what the lawman had said or was confirming that Marx was right. Then he said:

"She's waiting, fellers. And ladies don't like being kept that way."

"Please, Jase," Marx said in a whining tone. "While there's a life there's hope, uh?"

He tried to smile, but instead looked sick to his stomach with fear.

"Okay, Indian lover," Spenser growled bitterly and started forward, out of the crowd of people—Marx close to his side and Edge immediately behind.

"Gossip is all," the half-breed murmured reflectively. "We're just good friends . . . . I hope."

Chapter Twelve

NALIN HAD come to a halt on the trail just
before it reached the railroad crossing. She
looked as beautiful as he remembered her, but
not so fragile. Dressed in the same rawhide
skirt, but the shirt he had cut to examine her
wound had been replaced by a white blouse of
some fine fabric, city-styled for a white woman.
She no longer looked to be in physical pain, but
in the bright light of the now fully risen sun,
Edge was certain he could see mental anguish
in back of the firm resolve she expressed as he
gave a one-word order to halt the prisoners.
Twenty feet away from where she stood, the
same five hundred yards distant from her
people as the three white men were from the
grouped citizens of Calendar.

"How you been, Nalin?"

"Yellow Shirt and the braves are impatient,
Edge," she replied in a monotone, and he
thought she was having as much difficulty in

169

keeping emotion out of her voice as she had in avoiding a meeting of her eyes with his. "You will give us the murderers of our people and—"

"No he friggin' won't," Marx snarled, and gasped when the muzzle of the rifle was jabbed hard into the base of his spine.

"She knows enough bad English language, feller."

Nalin went on as if there had been no interruption: "—in return the white eyes from the train will be set free."

"To be buried, Nalin?"

Still she refused to meet him eye-to-eye. Kept the look of hatred on her lovely face as she answered:

"Nobody was harmed when the train was stopped. The white eyes you see displayed on the car were executed for wearing the clothes and adornments stolen from our camp. Everybody else from train is alive and well in the car. Will be exchanged for these son of a bitch murdering bastards."

"See what you mean about her language, mister," Marx said, his confidence expanding by the moment.

"Best you keep that overworked mouth of yours closed, Eddie," Spenser growled as, like the half-breed, he saw a look of puzzled suspicion dilute the hatred on the beautiful face of the slender young girl.

"You killed a few and hurt some more when you ran the engine into town, Nalin," Edge said.

"The extent of damage could not be foreseen,

white eyes," she answered. "But locomotive is sent as a warning. We will stop at nothing until murderers of our people are punished. You have brought them to me as prisoners. You give them to me now."

"What's happenin', Edge?" Cy Meek roared.

And Yellow Shirt raised his hands to cup them at his mouth and yell an equally short demand at Nalin in the Arapaho language.

"Your people and mine both grow more impatient, Edge," Nalin said. "Why should more time be wasted with words? You know that I am not well regarded by my people. Should I succeed in this, perhaps it will be better for me. But the patience of Yellow Shirt is exhausted, the fact that I am here with you and murderers will not prevent—"

The Arapaho chief made another demand—which took longer to express in a harsher tone than before. The girl's slender body stiffened as she listened. And her tone was tremulous when she warned:

"He says we have until the shadow on his pony's head grows shorter by the length of the ear."

"Edge?" Meek bellowed, sounding almost as angry as Yellow Shirt.

"Couple of minutes at the most, sheriff!" the half-breed shouted, without turning around. Then lowered his voice to accuse: "It's my belief you're lying to me again, Nalin."

"Never knew a woman that didn't do a lot of that," Marx put in evenly. But there was sweat on his face and the sun was not that hot.

"You just got to keep making with the mouth, don't you Eddie?" Spenser complained.

"If you think this of me, you have only to wait this short time for the killing to begin, white eyes!" the girl warned, voice harder than her expression.

"My guess is that the bodies strung up on the outside of that car are samples of what's inside of it."

"No!"

"Okay, move it again, fellers."

"Edge?" Marx asked, shrill with fear again.

"Come on, Eddie," Spenser urged as he started forward, onto the railroad crossing. "We got no damn choice!"

"I wish I was religious so I could pray," the smaller man moaned as he came up alongside his partner.

"Religious like a Trappist monk would be good," Spenser growled.

"Edge, I wasn't makin' no idle threat!" Cy Meek roared.

All this while the hand that Yellow Shirt had raised in the air remained poised, the Arapaho chief holding back from giving the signal until he was sure of Edge's intention.

Of the group of four at the intersection, Nalin was suddenly the most nervous. Certain that this situation was not as it seemed—and uncertain of how she should react to it.

"Girl!" Edge said, low but harsh, as the distance between the prisoners and the Arapaho narrowed to ten feet.

"Please!" she begged, and there was glistening moisture in her eyes.

"Mister?" Spenser rasped.

"Run like hell or go to it!" Edge said coldly, as he slid the Colt into his holster, shifted the aim of the Winchester away from the back of Eddie Marx and squeezed the trigger.

There was a smell of powder burn as the length of rope linking the two traders was blasted apart. At the same moment that the arm of Yellow Shirt streaked down, his hand curled to draw his rifle from the boot—as his braves made haste to get their rifles off their backs.

Spenser was the first to whirl and run back toward town, venting a string of curses. But his partner was close behind him, weeping and wailing. Both of them moving awkwardly, hampered by having their wrists tied at their backs. The girl was the last to start to swing around—her look of anguish showing that she was still torn by indecision. But then the dilemma was solved for her—when Edge encircled his free arm around her narrow waist and raised her meager weight up off the crossing. Held her tight against his hip as he turned and lunged in the wake of Spenser and Marx.

All this in the space of no more than five seconds. Then the first shot fired in the wake of the one that blasted the rope apart sent a bullet cracking past Edge's head—from town toward the Indians. And just a part of a second later two fusillades of shots exploded a hail of

bullets in both directions. But something close
to a thousand yards separated the opposing
groups. And there was something over half
this distance between the Arapaho and their
prime targets—lengthening by the moment as
the three men, all hampered to some extent,
ran for their lives while the Indians held back
electing to fire over such a long range from the
bases of stationary rather than galloping
ponies.

Nalin began to struggle—wriggling her body,
kicking her legs and flailing her arms. But she
was facing away from the man who held her so
easily and none of the attempted blows struck
home with force. He could hear her voice,
though, as she shrieked at him in her own
tongue and in English—the words he under-
stood certainly were curses.

Edge saw that the two traders were still on
their feet and running—zig-zagging by design
or perhaps made to stagger by not having the
balancing influence of swinging arms. And
maybe fear and lack of physical fitness also
played a part.

The second volley of gunfire from behind the
running men was less intensive than the
opening one—the braves with the single shot
rifles needing to take the time to reload. But
there was a continuous barrage from the
townspeople, as rifles and revolvers both were
triggered, cocked and triggered again. Every
barrel canted into the air to direct the blaze of
fire high. To avoid hitting the lumbering
runners whose retreat the constant shooting

was designed to cover—but the rising trajectory upon which the bullets were started out also had the effect of lengthening their range through the always decaying arc of their travel.

But there was still little chance of even the best marksmen placing their shots accurately. And when Edge drew level with and went between Spenser and Marx with Nalin's attempts to tear free weakening, every Arapaho brave was still astride his pony. Their chief, though, had not given the command for them to advance into the hail of gunfire.

Edge, the Winchester clutched in his left hand while his right arm maintained its lock around the waist of the girl, got ahead of the two city-suited traders as they all drew level with the end of the depot platform. And he angled to the side of them, breathing hard and having difficulty in seeing clearly with eyes stung by the salt moisture of sweat. So he was careful to watch his footing as he went across the track, conscious of the danger of tripping on the rails or the ties. Then he was up on the platform, his booted feet thudding on the boarding. The sound echoed twice from behind as the other two running men followed his course.

The sound of gunfire seemed to fade into the distance—into two distances. The length of the platform, the twin rails gleaming in the sunlight and the trail—all converging in perspective—were blurred by sweat and darkened by the effects of approaching exhaustion. There was a very dark area beyond the end of the platform, the track and the trail. The darkness stabbed across with spurts of very bright color. And for an instant his mind grasped at the reality of the image that had to be the big gathering of Calendar people who were blasting a barrage of shots at the Indians.

But then the idea he had briefly touched was set free again. And he was concerned only with getting himself and his burden over the final few yards to the ornately gabled railroad station building.

And he was almost there . . . .

The Indians were Arapaho, but that was immaterial to those white people who were directing a hail of gunfire at them. Calendar people nurtured a long-standing hatred for the Indians, whatever their tribe. So would welcome the opportunity to do just what they were doing now. That had been part of his plan. Part of his plan, too, had been to make the pair of traveling traders suffer for what they had done to the defenseless Arapaho at the Dora Spring encampment. Not by handing them over to the untender mercies of Yellow Shirt and his band of angry and grieving braves. But to get them up so they had a good chance of getting killed, and a better chance than the Indians they had slaughtered, of surviving. And in the process of this, he had to run the same risks himself.

He reached the station building, seeing only it and hearing just the thud of bullets into its walls. And then he was at the door at the center front of the building. Where he staggered to a halt, turned and fell against rather than charged at it. Felt it give way, folding back from him with an ease he had not expected. And he went across the threshold in its wake— one foot sliding to the left and one to the right. He went down hard and heavy—needed to use the rifle and his other hand to keep himself from crashing into a truck laden with crates, and could achieve this only by releasing his grip around the waist of the girl. She hit the floor with a cry of pain as he started to rise with a grunt of anger. Just as Jason Spenser and Eddie Marx plunged in through the doorway, to curse and shriek as, one behind the other, they tripped over the writhing girl and pitched to the floor.

The anger of the half-breed as he swung around and took three strides to reach the open doorway was directed inward. It was crazy. It had been crazy at the start and it had got to be crazier as it went along. The Arapaho squaw was nothing to him, yet against her will he had helped her. She was still nothing to him and yet he had put his life on the line because of her ever since he reached this town. Making the bastards pay for the massacre at Dora Spring, hell. It was for hurting Nalin he had got himself involved. And it was to keep her from being hurt again—or more likely killed—by the Indian haters of Calendar that he had got himself even more deeply involved now.

For a beautiful young girl who was nothing to him. Meant nothing to him . . . in the usual way of such male-female attraction.

"Shit!" he snarled against the continued barrage of gunfire with the occasional thud of a bullet into the outside walls of the safe refuge he had found for himself and his charges. And, as had happened so often during his life, he had the perfect outlet for an anger that otherwise might have turned from ice cold to white hot and exploded to no good account.

It had been inevitable that the man called Edge should abandon the girl rather than the Winchester after his crashing entry into the passenger waiting room of the station building. Inevitable, too, that he should recall despite the emotional turmoil within his mind that he had pumped the action of the repeater after firing the shot that severed the rope tying the two traders together. So that, as he stepped onto the threshold of the open doorway, the stock of the Winchester was against his shoulder, his cheek was resting on the stock and his forefinger was curled to the trigger.

He exploded a shot, worked the lever action and fired another. Then a third and a fourth. Too far away from the Indians to take careful aim. But satisfied to play his part in keeping them up near the bluff. Then driving them to take cover behind the corpse hung railcar after an occasional shot—whether from his rifle or the guns of the townspeople it was impossible to tell—had found human flesh and tunneled deep into it.

Here and there, a Calendar citizen had been hit by a stray bullet from an Arapaho gun. And this caused the whites to seek cover, too—behind and in buildings. So that the range was now almost impossibly long or there was no vulnerably visible targets to aim at. The barrage lessened, the shooting became sporadic and then finally ceased.

The silence that came to Calendar and the country to the north of it seemed to have a solid presence in the air, far less ephemeral than the gunsmoke that drifted through it and tainted it until the freshness of morning neutralized it.

"It is over now, white eyes," Nalin said, quietly and coldly after Edge had looked from the Indian positions to those of the whites. How long after the end of the gun battle he could not judge. Except that time enough had past for first a couple of whites then four Arapaho to venture out into the open and recover their respective dead.

"I wouldn't bet on it, girl," the half-breed answered as he made to glance over his shoulder at her. Then did a grimacing double take at her when he saw it was a statement she had made, not a question asked.

For a stretched second he thought she had been wounded again, for there was an ugly crimson stain on the frilled front of her rich woman's blouse. Blood on her hands, too. But then he saw the knife clutched in one of the blood-run hands. And his slitted eyes under their hooded lids looked to the left and right of

where she knelt on the floor of the station
waiting room in front of the crate-laden truck.
Saw to her left Jason Spenser and to her right
Eddie Marx. Both with their hands still tied
behind their backs, both with their throats
slashed open from ear to ear. The first killed
without the second one being aware of what
was happening. Each of them wearing a death
mask of exhaustion to show that the end had
come totally unexpectedly before they had
time to recover from their dash to cheat it from
another source.

"It is over, I say," she reiterated, without
moving and without altering the look of mild
satisfaction that was on her almost blemish-
free face.

"They had their hands tied. I tied their
hands, Nalin."

"The old men and the women and the
children and the little babies did not need to
have their hands tied to be helpless."

"Edge?" somebody shouted and the half-
breed had to think for a moment to recognize
the voice of Cy Meek.

"I have proved myself worthy to be an
Arapaho squaw, white eyes!" She seemed
oddly disappointed for a moment—perhaps because she was not able to inject as much
vehemence into the claim as she would have
wished.

"And proved me a bigger fool than I
thought, Nalin," he answered. Then swung the
rifle, pumping the action as he did so, and
squeezed the trigger the instant it was aimed

at her heart—as if he did not trust himself to make the right decision should he consider the problem a moment longer.

The bullet from such a high-powered rifle exploded over such a short range penetrated through her slender body, to burst free at the back and come to rest in the side of the truck. She had hit the truck with her back by then, bounced forward and then tilted to the side. Was dead with her beautiful eyes still open and the look of mild disappointment still spread over her lovely face.

"Edge, what the hell is goin' on down there?" the Calendar sheriff yelled, his anger expanding.

All attention—white and Indian—was focused on the open doorway of the station building during the several stretched seconds of silence that followed Meek's demand. Then guns were swung, fingers to the triggers, when movement was seen on the threshold. And a double chorus of chattering talk erupted at the north end of the two street and the vicinity of the railcar. Sparked by the sight of the sheepskin-coated, Stetson-hatted Edge emerging from the doorway. No longer carrying his rifle. Instead, dragging by the scruffs of their necks the bodies of Marx and Spenser.

For a second or so, all talk was curtailed. Then shock was vented by the whites as they saw the gaping wounds in the throats of the men. There was no audible reaction to the sight from the Indians.

"I warned you, Edge!" Meek roared.

But the half-breed had turned his back on the town and the whites, as he released his hold on the two corpse and made two passes with the side of his hand across his own throat. Then pointed to the dead men sprawled at his feet on the platform and shouted:

"Nalin!"

Which was sufficient. For without taking the time to think about what he had seen and heard, Yellow Shirt ordered his braves to withdraw. Back the way by which they had come toward Calendar behind the hurtling locomotive under cover of darkness. Now leaving behind the railcar with its hanging dead as they galloped their ponies without stealth through the early morning shadow cast by Trio Bluff.

"Edge, damn you, I want an explanation!" Sheriff Cy Meek roared as he started to lead a group of men out of town. A far smaller group of citizens than had been ready and willing to kill the Arapaho. All of them, including the lawman, had put up their guns.

"Marx and Spenser just found out that dealing in Indian artifacts can be a real cut throat business, feller," the half-breed replied as he moved back into the station waiting room.

"Goin' to check out the railcar, mister!" Meek called in as he and his deputy Hans Linder and Cecil Downing, the undertaker, past by and headed on toward the bluff.

And came back a lot faster than they went out. All of them with the exception of the German bartender hurrying on by the depot, Cy Meek bellowing that he wanted volunteers to form a posse to go after Yellow Shirt and his band of murdering Arapaho.

From the doorway, the short and fat, pale and balding, sad-faced man asked:

"Tell me something, please?"

Edge was sitting on a chair, a cigarette not quite forgotten at the side of his mouth for it wisped smoke every now and then. The frail and beautiful Arapaho squaw now lay along three chairs that were placed side by side in front of him. He had closed her eyes, but had not covered her. He held her hand as he stared down at her lovely face, concentrating on the small scar that marred her complexion.

"How's that, feller," the half-breed asked without looking at the bartender with a large butted revolver pushed into a side pocket of his baggy pants.

"How is it you knew that the railcar held only dead and not living people, Mr. Edge?"

"About the only thing I knew that she didn't do well was to lie, feller."

"I see," Linder said, and this was also obviously a lie. Then the German become an American looked about himself, embarrassed for some reason and for another not able to move away. Asked: "You are all right?"

Edge stood up and carefully placed the dead right hand of Nalin on the left one in the blood-stained frills of the expensive blouse.

"She was just a kid," he said as hooves thudded on the street down from the depot and horses snorted their eagerness to be moving.

"*Ja, das Kind,*" the man in the doorway

agreed absently. Then added with a start in the language of his adopted country: "A little child."

"So I'm fine now," Edge said coldly through teeth clenched and slightly exposed in a brutal grin. He picked up his rifle from where it leaned against one of the chairs on which the corpse lay and turned for the door. "But for a time there I was feeling a little stiff."

More bestselling western adventure from Pinnacle, America's #1 series publisher.
Over 8 million copies of EDGE in print!

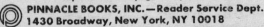